Edward Laight Wells

A Sketch of the Charleston Light Dragoons

From the Earliest Formation of the Corps

Edward Laight Wells

A Sketch of the Charleston Light Dragoons
From the Earliest Formation of the Corps

ISBN/EAN: 9783337254841

Printed in Europe, USA, Canada, Australia, Japan

Cover: Foto ©Raphael Reischuk / pixelio.de

More available books at **www.hansebooks.com**

OF THE

CHARLESTON LIGHT DRAGOONS,

FROM THE EARLIEST FORMATION OF THE CORPS.

———— ·· ————

PREPARED AT THE REQUEST OF

THE SURVIVORS' ASSOCIATION

OF THE COMPANY,

By EDWARD L. WELLS.

·

CHARLESTON, S. C.
LUCAS, RICHARDSON & CO., STEAM BOOK AND JOB PRINTERS,
130 EAST BAY.
1888.

A SKETCH

OF THE

Charleston Light Dragoons.

IT is a good rule, that every writing, however simple, should be held to "show cause" why it ought not to be burned, instead of being read. In a sketch of the Charleston Light Dragoons this "condition precedent" is readily fulfilled, for a corps, which has existed in this community for many generations, must be a subject of some interest. But there is a better reason than this; it is because the Dragoons were representative in a marked degree of the influences which made the Confederate army a grand body of citizen-soldiers. Aristocracy is a word now only to be spoken, if at all, under the breath, because it acts upon many as a red flag upon a bull; still, in spite of the risk of being gored, we will refer to Edmund Burke's statement to a British Ministry, to the effect, that the "colour-line" had made yeomanry, as well as gentry, at the South quasi-aristocrats, the outcome of which was a brave people devotedly attached to civil liberty. Of this state of society the Dragoons were, as has been said, peculiarly representative. Once, some one, as a joke, styled them the "kid-gloved company," but the imputation of dandyism implied, even if it had been true, would not have been very hard to bear. Wellington used to remark, as Croker says, that when he required a man for a specially difficult service, he looked around for one of the faces often seen peering from White's windows. In fact the dandy in all times has played an important part, particularly where the game happened to be war. As at Steinkirk, when the French army, surprised and routed, called upon the household troops to save the day, and gallants rustling in silk doublets, their lace collars hastily put on, sprang to arms; then the order rang down their line of battle. " Fire no shots! give them cold steel!" For once the Saxon went down before the Celt : heirs of the memories of Cressy and Agincourt before the splendid chivalry of France. Thus the dandies fought and throughout the land peasant vied with prince in gratitude to those " kid-gloved " companies, and all the pretty women for many a day wore lace scarfs knotted round their shapely throats in Steinkirk-fashion. What more could Frenchman want ?

If the story of the Charleston Light Dragoons is to be preserved, it is full time it should be written, for many of the facts exist only in the memories of the surviving members, and before long this detachment will hear the bugle-call to which they must yield obedience. The present sketch is intended to be confined to the " Old Company," to its personnel and memories, referring only to its regiment, brigade, or division where this is necessary to an understanding of the Dragoons' story. This is not done for the purpose of unduly magnifying the services of the Company, or of underrating those of others, but because the writer's information is too limited to warrant his entering a broader field. That the history of the cavalry of the Army of Northern Virginia will yet be written by the hand of the chieftain, who led its columns so ably, is earnestly to be hoped, and the greatest pride of the Dragoons will always be, that they were a fraction, however small, of Hampton's corps.

The story of the Charleston Light Dragoons is interwoven with the social and military history of South Carolina from early colonial days. It is to be regretted that public data in regard to its organization and personnel have been lost in the lapse of time, and that records of its own, old muster-rolls and similar archives, were necessarily abandoned, from lack of means of transportation, after its surrender with Johnston's army in North Carolina in April, 1865, at the end of the War between the States. It is clear that the corps existed at least as early as 1733, being called then with British loyalty the " Charleston Horse-Guards," a title changed, doubtless in deference to Republican sentiment, at the Revolution, into " Charleston Light Dragoons." *In 1733 Samuel Prioleau was captain, and some hundred and thirty years later two of his blood and name fought gallantly under the

colours—one brother being severely wounded at Pocotaligo, and
the other dying a hero's death at Cold Harbor. Similar recur-
rences among the Dragoons of family names indentified with
the "Horse-Guards" furnish circumstantial evidence that the
former was merely the successor of the original corps. Captain
Priolean commanded the company in the picturesque olden time,
the halcyon days, the golden-age of Carolina. Indigo and rice
were the twin-monarchs of agriculture, for that was long before
the democratic usurper Cotton was crowned king. Town and
country constituted a community practically one in blood and
interest. The banks of the Ashley and Cooper, the lands of
which Dorchester Church and those of St. Andrews, Goose-
creek and Strawberry were centres, were peopled by a prosperous and cultured gentry, and a brave and self-respecting yeomanry. Where at the present day you will see field and woodland torn up into an unsightly desert by the phosphate-diggers,
or ground once rich in agricultural produce now recaptured by
the forest; where now in some tangled covert you stumble upon
scattered bricks, or encounter in rude cabins tatterdemalion
negroes : in those same regions was formerly many a fine dwelling, fashioned after some hall in "merrie England," surrounded
by trim lawn or park, and many tinted garden. At the present
time, the old oaks, somewhat the worse for wear, and solemnly
bowing their gray beards of Spanish moss over the mournful
scene, are almost the only survivors, and the breeze through the
tops of the pines sighs, and whispers long tales of the past, of
pretty faces, and *beaux yeux*, of good fellows, and old Madeira.
Thus it was in the days of Captain Priolean, and later on, down
to the Civil War, the condition of things was not radically
altered, but only somewhat changed as to localities and details.
This was the state of society under which the Dragoons lived,
and for which, in our day, they died. On their muster-rolls, or
associated with them could always be found recurring such names
as Rutledge and Huger, Middleton and Priolean, Harleston
and Manigault, the cavalier commingled with the Huguenot
there, as he was in all social life.

In the stormy times of the Revolution the command is believed
to have consisted of several companies. This was the case in
1777, when Major Benjamin Huger, with a detachment from the
corps, rode out of the lines of Charleston to reconnoitre for the

expected approach of the British forces. Not having discovered the enemy in the vicinity, he was bringing his men back, and had reached a point in what is now Meeting street near the Citadel, when they were fired upon with grape from a field piece, in command presumably of some militiamen, who mistook them for the King's troops. Huger was killed. General Hampton, grandfather of the present General, at that time with the detachment, was riding "boot-leg and boot-leg," as he expressed it, with Major Huger.* The relative of this latter gallant gentleman, the inheritor of his name, and of the strong characteristics of the blood, fought under the flag of the Dragoons at Pocotaligo, Hawes-shop, and other hotly contested fields.

In a book of regulations for the militia of the State, under the date of 1794, is an elaborate frontispiece in which are blazoned the coats of arms of South Carolina and of the United States. On the right of the picture is a Federal flag, and on the left are two of the State, on one of which are engraved the letters C. L. D., from which it must be inferred not only that this corps was then of note, but that it was considered representative of the cavalry branch of the service.

There is extant a printed dinner invitation sent on June 27th, 1798, to Capt. Harleston, by " The First Troop Charleston Light Dragoons," which indicates that there was then more than one company in the organization.

In 1813 there were at least three troops of Charleston Light Dragoons, as the *Times* of that year gives the toasts drunk at a dinner by the "Third Troop." The length of the list makes one thirst for a share of the old Madeira, which must have flowed.

In 1822 the companies composing the corps were consolidated into one, and the number has never since been increased. At that time Captain Lynah commanded the "Drags," a charming gentleman of very fine personal appearance, and always well-mounted. From that date, up to the breaking out of the civil war, the organization was kept up in completeness, and with substantially the same material as had always figured in its ranks. It continued during those peaceful years its honorable existence, useful to the community as a guarantee of law and order, and ready to resume a warlike condition when the time

---

*This was related by Hampton himself to Hon. Alfred Huger ("The Post-master").

should come. Meanwhile, like the happy nations, its annals
have not been voluminous, and consist perhaps chiefly of recollections of dinners and suppers, and of the strict enforcement of
discipline against thrown riders, who were mercilessly fined, and
compelled to drink their full share of a dozen of Madeira, or a
basket of champagne.

Early in the spring of 1861, the Dragoons, as a militia company, commanded by Captain B. H. Rutledge, were ordered to
Sullivan's Island, where they performed with credit their duties.

The company, as State troops, marched from Charleston in
November. 1861, to Pocotaligo, on the Charleston and Savannah
Railroad, while Commodore Dupont, U. S. N., was bombarding
Forts Walker and Beauregard at Port Royal. Gen. Robert E.
Lee was then in command of the Military Department of South
Carolina, Georgia and Florida. After the reduction by the
Federal fleet of Forts Walker and Beauregard, the town of
Beaufort was abandoned by the inhabitants. The fall of the
forts was entirely unexpected by most of them, and therefore
they were obliged to hurry away from their houses quite unpre-
pared. Many were compelled to leave behind all their personal possessions, as they tore themselves from their pleasant homes forever, plunging from prosperity into life-long pov-
erty. A few days after this Gen. Lee sent Captain Ives of his
staff with a detachment of ten of the Dragoons to reconnoitre.
They crossed the Port Royal ferry, and rode into the town of
Beaufort. No Federal soldiers were occupying the place, and
everything there was quiet, although the negroes were in full
possession, their ideas of law and order not having yet been
completely "civilized away." A gun-boat was lying near at
hand looking quite harmless at the moment. The scene presented by the silent houses, with the evidences within and
around them of the sudden flight of their owners, was sad in
the extreme. The detachment returned to camp without experiencing any serious mishap, the chief result of the expedition
in a material point of view being a plentiful supply of poultry
"acquired" from abandoned residences, with which the troopers' saddles were loaded, their horses vigorously protesting by
many a snort, kick and plunge, as the unaccustomed trappings
dangled against their sides and between their legs. So the
Dragoons were the last Southern soldiers ever in the town of
Beaufort.

The company was ordered from Pocotaligo to Bee's Creek, a tributary of the Pocotaligo River, and assigned to picketing from there to Boyd's Landing. These picket-posts were intended to observe, and to cover, as far as practicable with such an inadequate force, the points at which the enemy could land from their fleet to cut the Charleston and Savannah Railroad, and thus sever the line of communication between those two cities. The purpose was of course a very important one, and the service required men whose personal intelligence and courage enabled them to be equal, when alone, or in parties of twos, or threes, to trying emergencies. A failure to discover, report to head-quarters, and thus thwart an attempted landing of the Federals, would result in great disaster. No "machine-made soldiers," manufactured by mere mechanical discipline out of an ignorant European peasantry, would be competent to perform efficiently a duty requiring in privates such a large fund of personal manhood. It was too a hard kind of service in many respects, the picket-posts being far from camp, and the fatigue and exposure great. But when in camp the Dragoons were "in clover," for most of them at this period of the war were in prosperous circumstances, some were wealthy: their messes were well supplied by foraging in the neighborhood, and by provisions sent from their homes: their servants, of which each man had at least one, were good, and some of the cooks excellent. With horses carefully groomed, and accoutrements in perfect order, the appearance of the command was very fine. No new members were admitted contrary to the wishes of the old ones, a system which was adhered to throughout the war, although it rested of course only on "unwritten law." The reputation of the "Drags" as a "crack corps," and the pleasant companionship to be found there, were very attractive, and resulted in a social composition probably quite unique even in the Confederate service, throughout which there was such a large proportion of well-born men in the ranks. Naturally there were frequently members being promoted to commissions in other commands, and then there would be officers disgusted for some reason with their positions elsewhere, and resigning them to enlist in the "Drags": so that it used to be jokingly said there was not a general-officer in the State, who had not been, at some time during the war, a member of this company.

Of all the messes in the company, that of Captain Rutledge and Lieutenant Nowell was notorious for always being the worst provided. One night these officers returned to camp very tired and hungry, having been engaged all day inspecting distant picket-posts. They called to their cook to give them dinner as quickly as possible, but when this appeared, it consisted of some rice and rice only. "Send in the rest," said the hungry men. "Ain't got no more, sah!" was the reply. But Jack observed a terrible storm brewing within those empty stomachs, conscious no doubt of having himself eaten what ought to have been kept for the dinner. "A woman scorned" is a dangerous thing, as the properly behaved scriptural Joseph discovered long ago, but a famished man may be worse. So thought the unscriptural Jack, and he cast around for some propitiatory excuse; a negro is never long at a loss for one.

"'Fore Gord, Mausa, *dat all;* but I gib yer somet'ing good *termorrer,* 'cus I git *contrack for one hog.*"

Imagine two starving fellows dining on a visionary, far off "*contrack* for a hog !"

"He may live without love,—what is passion but pining!
But where is the man that can live without dining ?"

General Lee's head-quarters were at this period at Coosaw-hatchie, about seven miles from the camp of the Dragoons, to which he paid a visit. The company went through a mounted-drill before him, at which he expressed himself well satisfied. He afterwards looked over the details of the camp, taking in everything apparently at once at a glance, and showing especial interest in the horses. Lieutenant O'Hear had a funny monkey called "Jack," who duly paid his respects to the General.

About the time arrangements were being made for reorganizing the company "for the war," Captain Rutledge and Lieutenant Nowell called upon General Lee at head-quarters in reference to the matter. The General was dressed in a plain blue coat, without brass-buttons, or any insignia of rank. Nowell relates that he was more impressed by his appearance, than by that of any living man he has ever seen, and it must be remembered that the interview occurred before the blaze of glory had been kindled, which afterwards immortalized Lee's name among all nations, and made it a sacred word in every Southern household. After their business with the General was finished, Cap-

tain Rutledge and Lieutenant Nowell left him, and went into
another room, where they met the members of his staff. Major
Washington, and Captains Ives, Taylor and Manigault were
present, and perhaps some others. A pleasant chat was had
with these "lesser lights," and some of the "wine of the country" was discussed.

During a very "cold snap," which occurred that winter, the
colonel of a North Carolina regiment of infantry camped near
the Dragoons invited Lieutenant O'Hear to accompany him in
a boat down Bee's creek to inspect the obstructions lately arranged near the mouth to prevent Federal gunboats from
ascending. Accordingly the party, consisting of some eight
persons, rowed down to the obstructions, and then pushed on
further, getting into the Coosawhatchie river and proceeding
until they arrived opposite Mackey's Point, upon which they
observed some soldiers. Now these North Carolinians were
"green" about salt water, unacquainted with the topography of
the country, and they took it into their heads that the people
whom they saw on the Point were a party of the enemy, and
these they were bent upon bagging. Anyone who has had some
experience of the tortuous navigation through marshes, well
knows how easy it is to get "turned-round" in one's ideas of
direction, and will understand the Colonel's mistake, for the
men on shore were only a picket from a Tennessee infantry
regiment. Lieutenant O'Hear, being "to the manner born" of
Southern salt-marshes, did not fall into the North Carolinians'
mistake, but was unable to convince them of their error, and
nothing would satisfy them but an immediate attack. So they
rowed towards the shore for this purpose, the Tennesseeans
meantime preparing the "compliments of the season" and a
warm welcome, for, equally ignorant of the localities, they mistook them for Federals, and were sure a landing in force was to
be attempted. Not very far from the shore the boat grounded,
and then the Tennesseeans opened fire in real earnest, the entire
picket-post turning out in fine style. The minies whizzed and
hissed and screeched persuasively around the ears of the North
Carolinians : it may have been "long between drinks," but was
not so with shots : it soon became a case of the hunter hunted ;
so all hands laid flat in the bottom of the boat, which managed to float away, and get to the other side of the marsh after

awhile, where they were glad to remain concealed until dark. By this time it was very cold, a cutting wind from the sea pouring over the open space in a way that will be appreciated by those who may have been belated in similar localities. But unfortunately the boat proved to be aground, and as it was found impossible to get her off, there seemed no alternative but to await with chattering teeth the flood-tide. However, O'Hear determined, in preference to this, that he would try to make his way on foot across the marsh to the nearest land, about a mile distant. Cut up, as the intervening space was, with innumerable small crooked creeks, the mud soft and tenacious, little better than quicksand, and with no guide in the darkness but the stars, it was not an easy undertaking. He offered to pilot those of the party, who chose to trust themselves to him, and set out accompanied by three or four. Some hours afterwards a silent figure emerged from the darkness, and glided up to a fire in the Dragoons' camp. He was hatless, with muddy water streaming from his hair, in dilapidated drawers, with trousers knotted round his neck like a scarf, and his neat velveteen shooting-coat a mass of dirt. This woe-begone apparition was O'Hear, and though very much liked by everyone in camp, nobody could possibly help laughing at the droll figure he cut. When able to speak, he told his friends of the poor fellows who had tried to follow him through the marsh, and who were lost there. Large fires were at once lighted along the shore, and by means of these after awhile the stray sheep, one by one, found their way out of their veritable "slough of despond," and the men in the boat turned up early in the morning not much the worse for wear. As for O'Hear, the "Drags" administered to him a large prescription of hot whiskey-punch and rolled him up in blankets, and the next day he was as jolly as usual, and as fresh as a lark. But the Tennessee picket was in dead earnest, and reported to head-quarters that the enemy had attempted to land. When this was communicated to General Lee by Major Washington, he remarked to the latter in his quiet grave way, "I think there is some mistake about this. The Charleston Light Dragoons are picketing in that neighborhood, and they would have reported before now any attempt to land."

During the latter part of March, 1862, the Charleston Light Dragoons, as an independent company, were mustered into Confederate service "for the war." The officers were :

B. H. Rutledge, *Captain*.
R. H. Colcock, *1st Lieutenant*.
L. C. Nowell, *2nd Lieutenant*.
J. W. O'Hear, *Junior 2d Lieutenant*.

The muster-roll of the non-commissioned officers and privates was :

NON-COMMISSIONED OFFICERS.

J. E. Harleston, *First Sergeant*.
J. C. Bickley, *Second Sergeant*.
B. F. Huger, *Third Sergeant.*
E. N. Ball, *Fourth Sergeant.*
J. H. W. Hutchinson, *Fifth Sergeant.*
S. W. Simons, *First Corporal.*
J. A. Miles, *Second Corporal.*
L. R. Bostick, *Third Corporal.*
Alex. Rose, *Fourth Corporal.*

PRIVATES.

Barnwell, F. M.
Bee, James L.
Bell, William
Bostick, Edward
Bostick, R. F.
Burnett, H. D.
Burnett, B. R.
Clark, J. M.
Chisolm, J. M.
Colcock, T. H.
Creighton, James
Davis, W. R.
Desel, C. M.
Desel, J. B.
Dupont, B. C.
Dupont, T. B.
Elliott, T. O.
Fairly, W. H.
Fitzsimons, P. G.
Fludd, Daniel

Freer, J. H.
Frierson, J. J.
Fuller, H. M. Jr.
Gaillard, E. T.
Gordon, A. B.
Gregorie, A. F.
Gregorie, W. D.
Gregorie, Isaac
Happoldt, John
Heyward, J. K.
Holland, E. C.
Holmes, E. G.
Holmes, T. G.
Huguenin, A.
Jenkins, A. H. Jr.
Lance, W. S.
Lining, Thomas
Lining, Arthur
Manigault, G. E.
Manigault, A.

Marion, B. P.
Martin, J. M.
Martin, Vincent
Martin, Edward
Martin, W. A.
Maxwell, P. J.
Meetze, J. Y.
Middleton, F. K.
Miles, J. J.
McLeod, W. W.
McPherson, J. J.
Neyle, H. M.
Nowell, E. W.
O'Brien, T.
O'Neille, J. J. A.
Palfrey, J. C.
Pringle, M. B.
Prioleau, C. E.
Pritchett, G. E.
Purcell, James

Rhett, B. S. Jr.
Richardson, J. B.
Richardson, John
Robertson, Alex.
Robinson, John
Robinson, Arthur
Seabrook, Henry
Seabrook, Joseph
Simons, Ion
Thurston, J. G.
Vanderhorst, L.
Vincent, W. E.
Wagner, A. C.
Waring, J. R.
White, W. W.
White, J. D.
Wilkins, G.
Witsell, E.
Witsell, W. H.
Wragg, A. McD.

After this date the Dragoons continued performing the same duties as before, and in the section of country already mentioned. By this time General Lee had left the department for a more important field, and had been succeeded by General Pemberton, with Colonel W. S. Walker in command of the district from the Ashepoo to Savannah Rivers, in which the Dragoons were stationed.

In the latter part of April of this year the enemy had effected a landing, and pushed a column to within a mile and a half of the Charleston and Savannah Railroad near Pocotaligo, from which point they retreated to their gunboats. They had been confronted by only two companies of mounted men—the Rutledge Mounted Riflemen and Nettle's Company, but the latter, being armed only with shotguns, proved of little use. The affair was a very trifling one in respect both to fighting and results, but it served to demonstrate the inefficiency, for that kind of service, of troops not armed with long range rifles.

Near the end of May, the Dragoons were assigned to picket duty from Bull River to Mackey's Point to cover the Charleston and Savannah Railroad, the line embracing Port Royal Ferry, which offered the enemy an easy means of approach, and from which they repeatedly made threatening demonstrations. The duty performed here by the company during this summer was of a very delicate nature and arduous. Their arms consisted only of sabres and pistols, supplemented by shotguns when on picket. The insufficiency of these weapons was a source of great anxiety to Captain Rutledge and his officers. The men, however, though often annoyed by the fire of the Federal pickets from the other side of the river at Port Royal Ferry, to which they were unable to reply, had in general a strong aversion to regularly carrying rifles, considering them unbecoming weapons for light cavalry. None the less did the officers endeavor to obtain the needed supply, but the authorities failed to furnish it, the scarcity of arms being one of the many difficulties with which the Confederacy had to contend. At length it was decided by Colonel Walker and Captain Rutledge, that Lieutenant Nowell should go to Richmond in the hope of procuring there the much coveted guns, but on reaching Charleston he unexpectedly obtained from General Pemberton an order for a supply, some Enfields having been received through the blockade. Great was the joy at company head-quarters when news of this success was received : so much so, that it was hardly credited, until the rifles themselves actually arrived. They were short Enfields, in length between that of a carbine and an infantry musket, and proved to be excellent weapons. Most of the men, as has been said, were very much opposed to being obliged to carry a kind of arm which they thought unsuitable and cumbrous ; they were "dead-set" against the "innovation." It was necessary, in spite of this, to issue the guns, which was accordingly done by Lieutenant Nowell. Each man marched up separately and received his weapon and cartridge box. Then it was a funny sight to see him leave. One would drag his rifle behind him, like a log ; another rode away on it in broom-stick fashion : a third shouldered arms "up-side down," and hung the belt of the cartridge box round his throat, like a necklace. All this was meant to express the contempt entertained by all genuine light cavalrymen for rifles, and their utter ignorance of the use to be made of such outlandish things. But there was destined, as will soon be seen, to be a through "conversion" on this subject: it seems, after all, majorities are not always right, treason though it be to say it, and the Enfields were hardly issued before their services proved of vital importance.

On October 22nd, 1862, the Charleston Light Dragoons were in camp at McPhersonville, about two miles from Pocotaligo Station on the Charleston and Savannah Railroad, near which were Col. Walker's head-quarters.

Early that morning the enemy effected a landing on Mackey's Point at the head of Broad River. Their force, under command of Gen. Brannan, numbered certainly not less than 2600 men, consisting of two brigades of infantry, a small detachment of cavalry, and some sailors, and a battery, and two sections, the artillery being mostly *Regulars. They had left Hilton Head the night before in gunboats and transports. A good road led from Mackey's Point to Pocotaligo (old Pocotaligo) about eight miles distant, on a river, or more properly speaking, a creek of the same, and thence to Pocotaligo station about two miles further. The Federals commenced before ten o'clock A. M. an advance up this road, which was covered for a certain distance by the gunboats. Their object was to seize the railroad at Pocotaligo station, destroying the small force there under command of Col. Walker, thus severing the line of communication between Charleston and Savannah, and placing both cities in jeopardy from a flank attack. As this line was about a hundred miles in length, and there were many places at which landings could be readily made under cover of gunboats, it was impossible to protect each point of danger by a separate adequate force, but, as long as the line of communication was preserved, troops could be dispatched, as needed, to threatened positions. The vital importance of maintaining the railroad intact is therefore evident.

Colonel Walker (afterwards General Walker, known as "Live-Oak Walker,") had to oppose to the Federals a force of 415 men of all arms, of which only 405 could be actually engaged after

---

*The force, said to number over 3000 infantry, besides artillery, was composed, according to the statements published at the time in the New York papers, of portions of 47th, 55th, and 76th Pennsylvania, 3rd and 4th New Hampshire, 5th and 6th Connecticut, 3d Rhode Island, 48th New York, part of 1st Massachusetts Cavalry, a section of Co. E., U. S. Artillery, and a section of Lieutenant Henry's Battery of 1st U. S. Artillery, besides a detachment from the New York Volunteer Engineers, and a Rhode Island Battery, and three howitzers manned by sailors. One regiment of the above named is said to have been detached to make a feint upon Coosaw-hatchie.

deducting the necessary horse-holders for the cavalry.* His artillery, consisting of eight guns—four from the Beaufort Artillery, and four of Latham's Battery, was under the command of Captain Stephen Elliot (afterwards the hero of Fort Sumter, and a brigadier general in the Army of Northern Virginia.) The Charleston Light Dragoons mustered that day some sixty men, as none were absent from camp on picket, but as the Rutledge Mounted Riflemen happened to be then on this duty, very few from that corps were available for the fight.

Col. Walker posted his command at Yemassee plantation, at a point about five miles from Mackey's Point, where the road crosses a marsh wet at high tide, but not impassable. Thin woods fringing the edge of the marsh on the left afforded but slight shelter to Capt. Elliot's four guns of the Beaufort Artillery stationed near the road. It was a beautiful autumn day and the enemy was marching gayly on in column of fours, without skirmishers, as if on a holiday street parade instead of being engaged in invading a country. They had got within very short range, about 75 yards, when Captain Elliot turned to Sergeant Fuller, whose stalwart figure was a living refutation of all the nonsense formerly heard about "effete Southerners," "Can you drop a shell in the head of the column, Sergeant?" said he. "I think I can," replied Fuller.

Bang! went the gun, and as neatly as one might put an orange on his plate at dessert, he dropped the shell into the desired spot, with fuse so nicely timed, that it burst just when it should, although the range was so very short, and thirteen poor devils were rendered hors de combat. Thus the fight opened, and the Federals, surprised apparently at an incident not down on the programme of a dress-parade, and disgusted at such rough horse-play, were for the moment a little disconcerted, but soon were formed in line of battle, and attacked.

The Dragoons had been dismounted to fight, and were near the centre of the line on the right of the road, their horses, as usual, having been sent back to a safe distance. The "conversion" spoken of had already been consummated; not a man would then have exchanged his hitherto hated Enfield for a fortune, for these were now making music pleasant to hear. They

---

*Col. Walker's Official Report. (Each fourth ["4th"] cavalryman has charge of the horses of the other three.)

were fighting on the edge of the marsh, the long rank grass being no protection from bullets, but serving fortunately to conceal from the foe their scanty number. The fire from the attacking columns was extremely heavy, but owing to bad shooting the balls generally went overhead. The Confederates, on the contrary, poured in steady well directed shots, which proved very effective. The Federals would again and again charge forward to within seventy or eighty yards of the Dragoons, fire a volley and then, in spite of the orders of their officers, would retreat a short distance : if they had realized the smallness of the force opposing them, of course they would have quickly run over the line. At length Gen. Terry, commanding one of their brigades, caught up the flag, rode forward gallantly and planted it within about seventy-five yards of the Confederate position, waved his sword, and shouted to his troops "forward." Sergeant Huger (Ben Huger) saw that the line could no longer be held, if Terry succeeded by his brave example in steadying his men; so he deliberately "drew a bead" on him, and pulled. Snap, went the cap without exploding the charge. He put on a fresh one, but it too snapped. Then he broke a cartridge, and with the powder carefully primed the tube, and placed on it a nice bright cap. There was still time, for Terry's men had not "enthused" very promptly, and there he was at point-blank range, less than eighty yards distant. He was a fine soldierly looking man, and was behaving gallantly, so that Huger had a great repugnance to killing him, but it must be done for duty's sake. Up came the rifle to his shoulder, and through the notch he saw the sight against the blue breast of Terry's coat, and pulled the trigger of his sweet shooting rifle. It snapped again, by all the Gods! Then the retreat began. T. M. Prioleau had been badly wounded, but his friends put him on a horse caught galloping by and thus he was saved. *Young Lieutenant Campbell, lately graduated from the Citadel Academy, happening to be in the neighborhood, had volunteered that morning in the ranks of the Dragoons, having borrowed a rifle from a horse-holder. He was shot dead, poor fellow. The memory of the brave boy has always had a warm place in their hearts. Here also O'Neill and Porcher were badly wounded, and Holland slightly hurt.

It had not been expected that this first position occupied by

*Daniel P. Campbell.

3

the Confederates could be held for any considerable length of time against the overwhelming odds attacking, but the object was to cause as much delay as possible to the progress of the enemy towards the railroad, and thus gain time for reinforcements to arrive, the urgent necessity for which had of course been telegraphed to head-quarters in Charleston early in the morning, when the pickets were driven in. The plan was now to withdraw to old Pocotaligo, between three and four miles distant, on the further side of a salt marsh divided by a creek about thirty yards wide and too deep to be forded, over which was a bridge. Here was the natural line of defence on which a final stand must be made. The withdrawal to this point was effected without much difficulty, as the Federals, instead of pushing forward boldly with their infantry, waited until a little bridge, crossing a part of the marsh at Yemassee, could be put in order for the passage of artillery. Having taken his force across the bridge into old Pocotaligo, Col. Walker had the planks torn up and formed his line to cover the creek. The main point to be held was where the road having traversed the marsh on a causeway cross ed at the bridge, because only there could the artillery be brought over, although infantry, if energetically handled, could have been thrown round Walker's right by marching to their own left and pushing through the head of the marsh, where the creek virtually ended in some wet swampy ground. A detachment of the Dragoons in fact crossed in this way, and rejoined their company on the further side of the creek. The enemy could also have struck the railroad, without crossing the creek at all, by leaving Walker on his right, and marching down a neighborhood road leading to Mr. Elliot's house, and thence going across some wet, yet quite practicable ground: but he was proba.bly unwilling to get away from his artillery, and to leave the Confederates in his rear.

The Dragoons were at first held in reserve back of old Pocotaligo, near the road leading to the station a mile and a half distant, but it was soon found necessary to order them to occupy the line near the bridge. "At the crisis of the fight," says Col. Walker,* "I ordered up the Charleston Light Dragoons. That gallant corps came forward with an inspiriting shout, and took position on my left, which wanted strengthening." Just at this

---

*Col. Walker's Official Report.

moment Lieutenant Nowell galloped up, sprang off his horse and took his place with the company, having reached Pocotaligo station a few minutes before on his return from Charleston, where he had been on leave.

The main body of the Federals was obliged to come to the attack across a narrow causeway leading to the bridge, or through the open marsh, and the casualties among them were comparatively large. But the disproportion of numbers was so excessive, that the Dragoons on the opposite side of the creek could not have lived under their volleys, if it had not been for the fortunate circumstance, that on their bank of the stream was a cluster of live oaks, which afforded protection in fighting. There is a natural affinity between brave men and oaks; in fact science would convince us, that all earth's flora and fauna are developed from a common germ, but however that may be, one is inclined to admit relationship to those grey-bearded aristocrats of the forest, who bared their sturdy breasts that morning to the bullets.

Referring to the Terry incident, it should be mentioned here, that Huger after crossing the creek, was about to undertake the troublesome business of drawing the bullet from his rifle, as it was spiked, but somehow it suggested itself to him, that before doing so, he would try another cap, although this appeared hopeless, as three had already been snapped without igniting the powder. So without priming, he put on a cap, pointed the rifle in the air, expecting no result, pulled the trigger, and bang! went the gun as clear as a bell. Now why was this? Chance? Gen. Terry might well entertain some old fashioned opinions about "a destiny, that shapes our ends."

*Col. Walker speaks in terms highly complimentary of the "cool and collected" manner in which Captain Rutledge ably handled his men under the tremendous fire, and also markedly commends the conduct of the company. It may serve to illustrate how thickly the bullets flew to mention, that the limb of a tree (from one of the brave old oaks), as thick as the upper part of a man's leg, was cut down by the minies. It was here that one of the "Drags," who was busily plying his rifle, called out in high glee to Rutledge, "Thank God! for the Enfields, Captain. I was dead against them, but now I say, bless God, and bless *you* for the Enfields."

*Col. Walker's Official Report.

Then he cheerfully sent another whistler into the mass in front.

One of the company was slightly wounded in the head; he instantly clapped both hands to his forehead, as if to ascertain whether the contents were there, and tested the working of the machinery by counting, "One and one make two, two and two make four," and then sang out, "'Thank God, the brain is safe," at which every one within hearing laughed.

The main road from Charleston united with that from Mackey's Point in open ground less than two hundred yards from the bridge.

The efforts of the Federal artillery were directed to taking up a position in the road beyond this point of junction, intending thence to sweep away the troops covering the bridge, which could then be repaired, thus enabling their column to cross. But Elliot's guns were magnificently served, and did handsome execution, and the Confederate sharpshooters would pick off the enemy's battery-horses, as soon as they emerged from the cover of the woods. Again and again the Federal artillery attempted to effect their purpose, but never succeeded, and the heaps of horses, and their many dead left at this point attested to the stubbornness of the struggle on both sides. After the fight the body of Captain Hamilton, commanding one of the batteries, was found at this place.

Col. Walker's force was reinforced by about two hundred men forwarded by railroad from Adams Run, who reached him after the final stand had been successfully made on the line of the creek, but as the fight was virtually won at this time, it may justly be considered to have been fought by the 405 men originally engaged.

The firing continued until about six o'clock P. M., when the enemy withdrew and succeeded in reaching his gunboats without material molestation from the Confederate pursuit. Along the line of his retreat however he left some six dead men, besides many coats, blankets, haversacks, and similar articles (according to his Virginia habit), thus showing that the withdrawal was hurried. The Federal loss is estimated by Col. Walker to have been over 300, which would be equal to about three-fourths of the Confederates in action, when the decisive part of the affair was fought. There is reason to think however that the Federal casualties much exceeded this number: but their reports are contradictory: *56 bodies were buried the next day, although the accounts published in Northern newspapers claimed that all their dead and wounded were carried off. The Confederate loss in killed and wounded was †145; no prisoners were lost, except five men captured on one of the picket-posts. The Dragoons out of about 45 dismounted to fight, had one man killed (Campbell,) and nine wounded— O'Neill, Prioleau, Porcher, Hopkins, Manigault, Holland, Pringle, Huger and Vanderhorst, the two last being very slightly hurt. This battle of Pocotaligo was remarkable for the disparity of the combatants in numbers, and for the fierceness of the fighting. The object the enemy had in view was of great importance, his purpose was entirely frustrated, and the punishment inflicted proved a discouragement to the repetition of similar attempts. For these reasons the battle is worthy of being remembered among the notable events characteristic of the War between the States, when victories were won against fearful odds by American soldiers warring with the heterogeneous mass composing the Northern armies. On such an occasion it was fitting, and in accordance with the saying "history repeats itself," that the names of Rutledge and the Charleston Light Dragoons should occupy a conspicuous place.

In the evening, soon after the retirement of the enemy, Capt. Rutledge joined Col. Walker on the other side of the creek, the planks having been replaced on the bridge. The Colonel was examining a haversack taken from the body of a dead Federal, and found in it a nice loaf of bread, which the provident defunct had doubtless intended for his own supper. One side of the loaf was discolored by the poor fellow's blood, but that part being cut off, Rutledge ate his share of the remainder with great gusto, washing it down with some "tonic" obtained from a good Samaritan. Immediately after this late lunch, Col. Walker ordered Captain Rutledge to mount his company, and proceed at once in the direction of Port Royal Ferry, to ascertain the position of the enemy, and to re-establish pickets at that place, if practicable. This was done, after a very distressing night march, the men being entirely without food for over twenty-four hours.

---

*Report of the Officer in command of the Burial Party.
†Col. Walker's Official Report.

After the events just described, the company continued doing picket duty as before, in the same section of country. It was while the Dragoons were stationed here, that an incident occurred. which impressed upon them the uncertainty of equine, as well as of human affairs. Among many fine horses owned by members of the company, was a mare of noted speed in a "quarter race" (a quarter mile dash). She had won so many matches, that now no competitors were left to her, and doubtless she often sighed at the thought that there was only one world to conquer. One day three men from another cavalry command called at the Dragoons' camp, and asked to be allowed to see this celebrated creature, a privilege readily accorded. The strangers were innocent guileless countrymen. They inspected the beautiful animal with interest, ran their hands with special attention over the hard swelling muscles of the upper parts of the hind legs, where resided the "driving power" essential to a spurt, and pronounced her "a fine thing." Then they timidly proposed a match between the mare and a horse belonging to their company, whom they would back to the extent of $100, but no more. Of course the bet was accepted, and arrangements made for the race, but it was not thought worth while meantime by the backers of the mare to look at her proposed rival, so confident were they of the result. The time for the meeting came, and a large number of spectators was present. When the Dragoons saw the countrymen's horse, a rough, thickset gelding, whose shaggy unkept winter-coat concealed the muscles beneath, they had compunctions of conscience at the thought of pocketing money on such an unequal contest. But when a verdant youth mounted the nag barebacked, preparatory to the start. they felt mortified at having been inveigled into such a ridiculous exhibition. The word was given, and away went the gelding. and won the race as if it had been child's play. "He laughs best, who laughs last." It came out afterwards that the winning horse did not belong to the guileless countrymen, but was a far famed "quarter horse," the conquering hero of many a Court House meeting. and had been brought from a distance to beat the mare.

In August, 1863, the company was ordered to Charleston. and camped at the Washington Race Course. During the siege carried on by Gilmore against Batteries Wagner and Gregg on

Morris Island, detachments from the Dragoons were sent there to act as couriers between the two forts. Morris Island, a narrow, irregular strip of sand, some four miles in length from south to north, lies at the southern entrance of Charleston harbor. About three-fourths of a mile from the northern end (that nearest to Charleston) was Battery Wagner, one of the outer bulwarks of the city. Battery Gregg, on Cummings Point, at the extreme northern end of the Island, distant about three-quarters of a mile from Wagner, was a much smaller fortification; in effect little more than an outwork of the latter on the line of communication with the city. The heroic defence of these positions against the land and naval forces of the Northern States is matter of history. But the names of Wagner and Gregg no longer have anything but an historic existence. The stranger finding himself on Morris Island near the present Life-saving Station, will be not far from where Gilmore first effected a landing, but the encroachments of the sea and the shifting sands have much altered the ground. Proceeding in a northerly direction, one will now pick up old minies, and notice many signs of the former occupation, in rusted cans, canteens, and cooking utensils, with an occasional fragment of a rifle-barrel, or bayonet. Walking on still further in the direction of Wagner, he will often observe the toes of shoes projecting from the loose sand, which the winds alternately pile up and strip from the skeletons beneath. The bones are much disintegrated by the action of the atmosphere and salt water, but, strange to say, the *jaw-bones* are best preserved, from which one may draw a moral to suit his taste. The presence of good shoes on a dead man would indicate to any "old Confederate," that these remains were once Federal troops, and such they were ; these thousands were the "chips" in the "game of war," the price which Gilmore paid for the evacuation of the fort. But when you reach the spot where Wagner once stood, you will realize that the forces of nature are more irresistible, though less cruel, than man, for the ocean has wiped out nearly all vestiges of the once powerful fortification, which the Federals were unable to destroy, but the breakers, if it be high tide, will be rolling in, moaning and groaning for the dead, and spreading snow-white winding sheets of foam over what remains of this place of glorious memories. As for Gregg, the very point on which it stood, has been devoured by the waves. All these things will set you reflecting and moralizing, unless you are a veritable Gradgrind; as you look across at old Sumter, you may well feel that your feet are treading holy ground, and you will be a better man for the thought, wherever your home may be, or whatever your political sentiments.

It has been said in *accounts written of the siege of Wagner, that the courier duty there was performed by detachments from the Fifth S. C. Cavalry, but this is an error. The Fifth was engaged in this service up to August 20th, when they were relieved by the Dragoons, who remained in it during the last seventeen days of the bombardment, up to the completion of the evacuation. The first forty days of the siege were no doubt frightful, but the last seventeen were of course necessarily much worse, just as a pot becomes hottest as it nears the boiling point. On the 21st of August, the parallels had crept up to within 300 yards of the Fort, and the sappers had dug their way to the moat by the evening of September 6th, when the position was evacuated.

The duty being considered especially dangerous, the details for it from the Dragoons were selected by lot. The first detachment, consisting of ten men, under command of Sergeant Benj. F. Huger, was ordered to Wagner on August 20th. It was necessary to go from the city by row-boats at night: this was the only mode by which the Fort could be supplied with reliefs of men, as well as ammunition and food, and thus the wounded were brought back. During daylight all the water approaches were liable to be swept by the Federal gunboats. The Dragoons landed at Battery Gregg, where quarters were assigned them in a little bomb-proof into which they could barely squeeze. Just behind this place, in comparative security, their horses were fastened, always saddled and bridled. These animals, five in number, were left by the couriers, whom the Dragoons relieved, the latter not bringing with them any horses. Huger placed a list of all the men, including his own name, on the inside wall of the bomb-proof, and they were to ride in the order fixed, he taking his turn regularly; this was voluntary, for, being in command, he was exempt from this duty. Always before mounting to carry a dispatch, Huger appointed a man to command until his return, or in case of his death. The duty of the couriers consisted in carrying dispatches, received from the city via Fort Johnson by boat, to Battery Wagner and bringing from there dispatches intended for the town, as well as in riding with communications verbal and written between the commandants of Wagner and Gregg. For these purposes two couriers were always stationed at the former fort, the rest at the latter. Important dispatches were forwarded by two men, one starting a little later, so as to guard against the loss or delay in transmission, which would otherwise be caused by the death of the first sent. It was impossible to communicate between the forts with sufficient rapidity by any other means than mounted couriers, and it was necessary for these to ride along the beach, as the loose sandhills further from the water would render locomotion very slow. When a man received a dispatch or an order to carry from Gregg, he would lead his horse to near the end of a curtain-wall running down to the front beach, mount him, and then turn the animal round the corner of the wall. Nothing else was needed: neither word, whip, nor spur; as fast as he could run, the horse would dash down the beach and make straight for an old gun-carriage under a projection of the wall near the sally-port of Wagner where he was accustomed to be tied. Nothing but contact with shot or shell could prevail upon him to slack speed, until he reached this place, for he well knew that it was a race for life. On leaving the cover of the curtain at Gregg, horse and rider were at once exposed to the projectiles from the fleet, which was continually pounding away, and of course became a special target. The big shells, 100, 200 and 300 pounders, would come along with their horrible shriek often striking the sand, and ploughing out a deep hole, then ricochetting and cutting huge trenches in the opposite marsh. The distance between the forts was about three-quarters of a mile, and at about a quarter of a mile from Wagner the course along the beach turned a little to the right, which brought one in full view of the fort; this stretch was fearful, for here one not only plunged among all the big shells hurled at the fort from ships and land batteries, but amidst the little perpendicularly-dropping Cochorn mortar-shells too, and also the minies from the sharp-shooters in the rifle pits. The fellows used to stand in the sally-port of Wagner to watch the

4

riding. They would cheer and yell and leap and dance in excitement, as they saw horse and rider coming. When these got through safely, they would often catch up the man as ho dismounted, and laughing and cheering carry him on their shoulders into the sally-port. But when a rider was wounded or thrown by a horse falling, these same devil-may-cares would run out into the fire unhesitatingly to pick him up and bring him under cover. The way in which the last quarter, the "home-stretch," was made was a sight to stir the blood of the most phlegmatic; the "fires of hell" pouring around, the horse running, as never horse ran before, the rider leaning down against the mane to present least surface to bullets, and dozens of spectators cheering wildly. On one of these occasions a looker-on among the sandhills exposed himself carelessly; a large shell struck him in the body, literally scattering the corpse in fragments, which had to be picked up by his friends in a wheelbarrow for burial. Of all the horses, a little flea-bitten grey was the favorite. He would leap off at full speed and run steadily and low in a thoroughly business-like way. The poor animal became bobtailed through the summary operation performed by a shell, but afterwards ran even the better for the recollection of his mishap.

Burgess Gordon, of Huger's Squad, was carrying a dispatch, when a shell tore up a huge hole in front of his horse, going at full speed. The result was a somersault for both, but Gordon was not permanently disabled by the fall.' Others received injuries, but none of the detachment were killed. A relief squad from the Dragoons reported on August 30th. By that time the pot was near boiling point, and they therefore experienced even harder service than their predecessors. Taylor and Fairly were stunned by the explosions of large shells, and were sent up to the city. John Harleston was struck by a fragment of a shell and knocked down by the concussion, but remained on duty after reviving. Others were less seriously hurt. All of the horses were eventually more or less wounded; one was shot in the chest by a minie bullet. There was much suffering caused by a lack of water. The rations were limited and in very unwholesome condition, the heat being excessive. The stench produced by obvious causes within the Fort, and the smell of the putrifying corpses but partially buried in the sands outside, were sickening. All the while the enemy plied his land batteries, which were hourly being pushed nearer and nearer, and the Iron-clads kept hammering away, while the sharp-shooters made it death for any head shown above the parapet or through a crevice between sand-bags. A Georgian was heard to say just after the evacuation, "I ain't afeard of hell no more; it can't touch Wagner."

At length it was determined to evacuate Wagner, and Sunday night, September 6th, was fixed upon for the purpose. The object for which this fort had been up to that time held, had now been accomplished. An inner line of defences had been perfected, and Gilmore was foiled in his attempt to capture Charleston, a feat not destined to be accomplished by any Federal commander.

On Saturday night, September 5th, after a furious shelling of many hours continuance, Gregg was attacked by the Federals in boats. The usual garrison was about a hundred men, there being no room to shelter a larger number, but reinforcements had been sent from Wagner in expectation of the attack; these were stationed among the sand hills, which afforded a very in-sufficient cover from rifle shells, and none at all from mortar-projectiles. John Harleston and Charles Priolean from the Dragoons took rifles and fell in with a detachment from the 27th Georgia, a part of the reinforcements from Wagner. The enemy attacked in some twenty barges, advancing from the creek side, but were repulsed at close quarters with considerable loss, the rifles of the 27th Georgia contributing gallantly to this result, the two Dragoons just mentioned being part of the "orchestra."

On the night of August 6th, it will be remembered that the enemy had succeeded in digging his way up to the very moat of Wagner, whose guns pointing in that direction had long since been dismounted. It can easily be understood than an evacua-tion under such circumstances, the withdrawal of a garrison of less than a thousand men hemmed in by ten times their number of land forces supported by a large fleet of Ironclads, was a pro-ceeding of almost superhuman difficulty. So close were the hostile forces brought together, that the slightest sounds or movements of a suspicious kind within the fort would have betrayed the besieged to their vigilant foe. To prevent this a spirited fire was kept up to the last moment, silence in other respects being observed as far as possible. Gradually the troops were withdrawn from Wagner and marched quietly down to Gregg, from which point they were successfully removed in boats to the inner line of fortifications, so that when the Federals next morning were about advancing to make another of their assaults in force upon the position, the besieged were found "not at home." The Dragoons were kept very busy while the evacuation was going on, and only after all the detachments from Wagner had been brought off did they embark, among the last to leave the Island. The horses had to be left behind, a hard thing to do after they had served their country so faithfully, but the bridle belonging to the little gray was brought off as a memento, and the brave little fellow will never be forgotten.

Harleston had not been drawn by lot for the service on the Island, but had volunteered in place of a man, who, for reasons of his own, consented to let him go in his stead. Hardly had Harleston landed on the wharf in Charleston on returning before his friend rushed up to him, grasped his hand, and cried out, "Thank God, you are safe! If you had been killed, I would have been your murderer. However much *you* may have suffered during this last week, *I* have suffered more in realizing what I had done."

After the evacuation of Morris Island the Dragoons performed duty on the land-approaches to Charleston, and in April, 1864, were stationed at Accabee on Ashley River, about seven miles from the city. Previous to this Captain Rutledge had been promoted to the Colonelcy of the 4th S. C. C., and Colcock had become captain of the Dragoons, with Nowell 1st lieutenant, O'Hear 2d lieutenant, and Edward Harleston Junior 2d.

Here the monotony of their life was broken by a ripple of excitement; it was rumored that they were to be ordered to Virginia to serve in the campaign about opening. Soon the rumor assumed more definite shape, and at length all doubts were dispelled: the Dragoons, as Co. K., 4th S. C. C., were ordered to join the Regiment, which was to rendezvous at Columbia; the 4th, with the 5th and 6th S. C. C., would form a new Brigade for M. C. Butler, lately promoted to be Brigadier-General, and would march for Virginia.

The Brigade thus to be organized would be an important addition to the Cavalry of the Army of Northern Virginia. The three regiments had full ranks, and had been disciplined and accustomed to army life so long, that they might be considered, in some sense, as veterans. Moreover they were well mounted, each officer and private furnishing his own animal, according to the practice of the Confederate Army, and it was no small consideration to Government to secure such a body of fresh horses, as well as men, for the next Virginia campaign. It was true that these regiments could ill be spared from the defense of the coast of South Carolina, but they were still more needed by Lee's Army, where the cavalry had been much weakened in numbers and efficiency by the operations of the previous year, whilst that of their enemy had much improved. Butler's Brigade was intended to form part of the Division of General Hampton, whose system of manœuvring cavalry was different from that previously in vogue in Virginia, and indeed may be said to have been up to that time unique. Instead of using cavalry chiefly for raids, and desultory skirmishing, affairs too often more captivating to the fancy, than productive of substantial results, Hampton conceived the idea of making this arm terribly effective as masses of infantry, while losing none of its serviceable qualities as cavalry. Men in large numbers, who could be relied upon to fight, when dismounted, with the steadiness and tenacity of infantry, and who, being provided with horses, could move with much greater celerity than foot-soldiers, would be capable of being handled, it was thought, with telling effect, not only in covering retreats, or masking advances of larger forces, or forcing the enemy to "show his hand," but also in striking important blows on their own account at weak points. This conception of the practicability of widening the sphere, and increasing the importance of cavalry was carried into effect when Hampton, after Stuart's death, took command of these forces attached to the Army of Northern Virginia, and Butler's Brigade was destined to play an important part in this programme. Since the end of our War this idea, originated by Hampton, has become familiar to general military science, but at the time of which we are speaking, it may be said to have been a "new departure."

Butler's Brigade was armed with sabres and most of the men had revolvers, but the rifles carried by all were the important weapon. These were muzzle-loaders, throwing a minie-ball, while the troops they fought used breech-loaders. As soldiers provided with breech-loaders ought to be a match for double their number armed with muzzle-loaders only, the immense disadvantage under which Butler's and Young's Brigades, composing *Hampton's Division, labored in this respect, ought to be borne in mind in estimating their successes gained against fearful odds in men and *materiel*.

Early in the morning of April 10th the "Drags" commenced their march for the rendezvous at Columbia. No doubt there had been tender leave-takings in plenty, but on these it is needless to dwell, the chief reminiscence remaining being of a symposium on the night before the departure at which the reputation of the corps, as "honest drinkers," was well maintained. Whether it was this, or more sentimental causes, that made them wear unusually grave faces the next morning, may be a matter for doubt.

The company before leaving the coast had to be reduced to the maximum number fixed by law, there being at that time an excess, counting detached men. The members thus cut off were such as had most recently enlisted, but some of these volunteered " for Virginia," and exchanged with older members, thus remaining with the " Drags." A muster-roll of the Company, as thus constituted, follows, though *all* the names do not represent men who actually served with the colours in Virginia:

OFFICERS.

R. H. COLCOCK, *Captain.*
L. C. NOWELL, *1st Lieutenant.*
T. W. O'HEAR, *2nd Lieutenant.*
E. HARLESTON, Jr., *Junior 2d Lieutenant.*
T. C. BECKLEY, *First Sergeant.*
B. F. HUGER, *Second Sergeant.*

PRIVATES.

Adams, R.	Blake, W.
Adams, J. R.	Bostick, B.
Adger, Jas. Jr.	Bostick, L. A.
Bee, J. S.	Brisbane, J. L.

---
*Afterwards Butler's Division.

Boyle, W. A.
Bedon, Josiah
Bellinger, W. H.
Boone, J. W.
Burnett, B. R.
Bell, William
Chisolm, J. M.
Clark, J. W.
Davis, W. R.
Desel, J. B.
Desel, C. M.
Durant, T. W.
Dupont, B. C.
Elmore, A. R.
Evans. J. W.
Fairly, W. H.
Frierson, A. C.
Fishburne, W. H.
Freer, J. H.
Gregorie, A. F.
Gordon, A. B.
Holland, E. C.
Holmes. T. G.
Howell, J. M.
Hopkins, Jas.
Hutchinson, P. H.
Jenkins, A. H. Jr.
Kirkland, W. L.
Law, J. W.
Lining, A. P.
Lining, Thomas
Lewis, F.
Martin, R. H.
Manigault, Alfred
Manigault, G. E.
Manning, W. H.
Middleton, F.

Middleton, O. H.
Mikell, E. W.
Miles, J. J.
Miles, J. A.
McLeod, W. W.
Neyle, H. M.
Nowell, E. W.
O'Brien, T.
O'Hear, L. W.
Palfrey, A. C.
Porcher, P. R.
Pringle, J. R. P.
Pringle, M. B.
Pringle, J. J.
Pringle, D. L.
Phillips, A. B.
Prioleau, J. M.
Prioleau, C. E.
Richardson, J. B.
Richardson, H. W.
Richardson, R. C.
Robertson, E. R.
Robertson, Alex.
Robinson, Arthur
Robinson, John
Rhett, B. S.
Taylor, A. R.
Thurston, J. G.
Trenholm, E. L.
Vanderhorst, L.
Vincent, W. E.
Waring, M N.
Waring, J. H.
Wells, E. L.
Weston. R.
White, W. W.
Withers, W. R.

Wragg, A. McD.

On the route to Columbia, at Branchville, a junction was

made with the regiment, the 4th S. C. C., Col. B. H. Rutledge commanding, formerly captain of the Dragoons.

At Columbia a review of the regiment was held by General Hampton, and the effect was quite impressive, for a thousand troopers mounted have the appearance of very much greater numbers than a body of infantry containing an equal quantity of men. The Dragoons were easily to be distinguished from the other companies by their superior uniforms, equipments, and horses. When the General galloped down the lines, looking every inch a chieftain, the air rang with the shouts of the soldiers, soon to be repeated in far different scenes.

The 4th Regiment was to go to Camden to have their horses shod, there being a supply of iron at that place, and thence to march for Virginia. The "Drags" on leaving Columbia were loaded with flowers, as well as with less sentimental gifts, and were continually waving farewells as they rode along the streets. At Camden quite an ovation was met with from the ladies, and more "refugee" friends found. There was another supper, too, with none of the fair sex present, but with oceans of old Madeira to sustain one's spirits in their absence. Recollections of matters and things towards the close are a little vague, consisting chiefly of lights and decanters dancing the can-can. As, however, this was the last of these "feasts," all the men becoming afterwards per force "total abstinents," the souls of Prohibitionists will no more be vexed by recitals of such levity. The line of march to Virginia for each of the three Regiments of the Brigade was different, thus facilitating the obtaining of rations and forage along the route. The quartermaster and commissary of course preceded the column for the purpose of making the necessary arrangements for rations and camping, and when the regiment reached their destination at night, it was occasionally found that the country people had got up a gratuitous "spread" for the boys, as best they could, and gave them kindly honest welcome. Frequently there would be, on the part of the entertainers, speechifying in the good old American Fourth-of-July-style of oratory, but the "Drags" could always give them a Roland for their Oliver in the person of a "silver-tongued" Sergeant. As for the hosts, being usually poor wounded fellows on furlough, or men too aged for the field, there was about them a mute eloquence often more effective than words. Sometimes the kind ladies, who had prepared the entertainment, would gratify their curiosity by looking through the camp, for a full cavalry regiment was a novelty in those rural places remote from the theatre of actual hostilities.   None of the men had tents, and very few of them possessed flies; most of them slept without any protection from the weather when it was clear, and in rainy nights a blanket stretched along a stick served to turn the water, india-rubbers not being owned until captured from the enemy.   This was the case until late in the autumn, so that the "tented field" was an incorrect figure. On one occasion an old lady, who was being shown through the camp, at length exclaimed, "But where do you undress?"   It had to be delicately explained, that a cavalry-man was supposed to be in *robe de nuit* when he had unbuckled his spurs.

The march was made with fresh animals through a country having plenty of forage, the average distance being twenty-five miles a day, and yet when the command reached Richmond many horses were temporarily unserviceable from sore backs. This shows the difficulty of keeping up the strength of cavalry, where a disabled horse means a useless man.   The Dragoons suffered less in this respect than the other companies of the Regiment, probably because they used better saddles.   Col. Rutledge foreseeing the mischief that would be done by defective saddles, had applied to the Quartermaster General at Richmond for a supply of the McClellan pattern, but this was not obtained until after arrival in Virginia, too late to prevent the trouble already caused, much of which might have been avoided.

When the regiment reached the neighborhood of Clarksville, Va., news came to head-quarters that Federal cavalry were on a raid through that section, partly intended, it was supposed, to gobble-up the Fourth, and that they might stumble on them at any moment.   This was startling intelligence, because, not only were the raiders reported to have a force several times larger than the Fourth, but the latter was without rifles, which had been shipped by railroad to Richmond, so as to lighten the load for the horses on the march, and to facilitate the men in leading those belonging to comrades furloughed, who were to report in Virginia.   The regiment was armed with sabres, and most, but not all of the troopers, were provided with revolvers; but with these alone to fight an enemy very largely outnumber-

ing them using breech-loading rifles, was an awkward undertaking. It was rather a ridiculous position to occupy, too, and
most of the fellows made merry over the situation in a devil-
may-care way: but to the officers, who felt the weight of the
responsibility resting on them, it was anything but a laughing
matter. There was nothing to be done under the circumstances
but to endeavor to avoid a collision, and if that proved inevi-
table, to make a quick mounted charge and ride down and cut
through the raiders. This latter alternative was perfectly practicable, but it might result in the loss of the wagon-train and
led-horses. The men of the Fourth were sturdy fellows, accustomed all their lives to ride, and had for two years been well
instructed in both the infantry drill and in sword exercise.

Accordingly the Dragoons were sent forward as the advance
guard. The regiment felt its way along cautiously, seeing no
blue-coats during the day, and at night put out pickets. The
enemy did not make an appearance, however, so the trouble
was taken in vain, but the incident proved a little excitement
to relieve the monotony of the march.

The Fourth in due course reached Richmond and marched
through the city, attracting no little attention as the regiment
was supposed from its numbers to be a brigade. The command
camped on the Brook Turnpike, about two miles from town.

And now comes the period when this sketch must contain accounts of hard fights, in which many valuable lives were laid
down. But those men died in defence of civil liberty, which,
though crushed for a time, was rendered possible afterwards by
the moral strength of the principles for which such as they fell.
Thus they did not pour out in vain

"The last libation Liberty draws."

The military movements in which they fell were parts of the
grand strategy of Lee, who never expended, without necessity,
the lives of his soldiers. On one occasion a collision occurred
between infantry out-posts, which, through undue zeal and
without sufficient military reason on the part of the Confederate officer in command, developed into an engagement in which
many lives were lost. The officer returning from the pursuit
of the enemy, by that time cooled down, and realizing bitterly
his blunder, came upon Gen. Lee sitting motionless on his horse

among the dead and dying in the sombre autumn twilight, a grand figure, but silent and grave. He rode up to Lee as if about to say something in excuse, but was stopped by the gently uttered words—

"Well! well! General! Bury your poor dead!"

Only those simple words, "your poor dead," but his look and tone contained the loftiest eloquence, expressed profound compassion. Then the men seeing General Lee, broke into deafening shouts, and the poor wounded fellows writhing on the ground tried to cheer.

A short time before the arrival of the Fourth in Richmond the enemy's cavalry had made a raid in the rear of Lee's position, and penetrated to a point very near the city. It was then that Gen. "Jeb" Stuart was killed at Yellow Tavern, by which event Gen. Wade Hampton became senior Major-General in the cavalry of the Army of Northern Virginia. He took command at a very critical period. The situation was alarming, for it was evident that Sheridan was numerically so very much the stronger that he would be able to raid in almost any direction at will. To this a stop must be put: not by counter raids, but by the hard infantry fighting of dismounted cavalrymen. Thus the arrival of Butler's and Young's Brigades from the South was looked for with great interest, for they were to be utilized without delay. As soon as the Fourth had arrived and reported at Lee's head-quarters, it proved advisable to strike Sheridan a serious blow, although neither of the two fresh brigades was complete, the 6th S. C. and some of Young's command not being as yet upon the ground. The neighborhood of Atlee's Station, on the Virginia Central Railroad, was at this time occupied by Grant's cavalry advance, masking his infantry manœuvres.

The Fourth remained camped two days on the Brook Turnpike, and when on the morning of the third day the march commenced for Hanover Junction only some 400 men were in saddle, nearly 600 horses being disabled, chiefly by galled backs. A halt was made about noon, and the regiment bivouacked in a wood about a mile in the rear of the Confederate position. Along the roads a great movement of wagon-trains was observed, caused by Lee's preparations to move from Hanover Junction in order to oppose his front to Grant, as the latter was endeavoring to execute a flanking movement to his left, which came to a disastrous end at Cold Harbor. The Fourth remained where it had halted until the next morning. In the meantime Col. Rutledge and his adjutant, Manigault, (formerly one of the "Drags") rode to head-quarters to report to Gen. Lee. They were told the General was indisposed, and therefore not to be disturbed except on urgent business: so their report was made to his adjutant, Colonel Taylor. Everything was simple and unpretending around the General's little wall-tent, the officers of his staff being quartered in a farm-house near by. There was no sentinel: only a few orderlies, or couriers, were seen, whose horses were fastened in the vicinity, and there was so little to distinguish the place in appearance that a stranger would have had some difficulty in finding head-quarters. Indeed many a soldier, of whom inquiries were made, was ignorant of the whereabouts of the General-in-Chief. What momentous thoughts must have been passing through his mind, as he lay there in his tent apart from all mortal eyes! His was the genius that was then transforming meagre battalions into a bulwark against odds apparently absolutely overwhelming from the physical weight of numbers.

The next morning the Dragoons ate a very slim breakfast, all that their negroes, lords of the frying-pan, would allow. These servants proved tyrants of the most merciless kind in Virginia, where only the limited army rations intended for the men could be obtained. On the coast of South Carolina it had been different, for there these could be supplemented by bought supplies. In Virginia the usual daily allowance to a man was one-third of a pound of bacon and some corn-meal, occasionally varied by wheat-flour, there being no coffee, tea, or other stimulant. As the servants of the messes took good care not to starve themselves, it followed that the digestive organs of their masters had but little employment. This soon necessitated a reduction of camp-followers, but in the meantime much needless suffering was incurred by the men.

The negro servants were always fertile in excuses for lack of food, although there were but too often good reasons for the deficiency. On the occasion of a halt on the roadside between Frazer's farm and Mechanicsville, where the men of the regiment received government McClellan saddles, one of the "Dragoons," who, like all the others, was already suffering from chronic hunger, while looking around for some stray crumb that might be in sight, accosted the usually sleek and well-conditioned servant of Surgeon Gregorie, of the Fourth, Othello by name. Knowing his skill as a cook and provider, and that the interests of his master were usually uppermost in his mind, he inquired whether a morsel from his haversack could be spared him. The "Moor," though contrary to his usual habit, for he was naturally cheerful and civil, looked moody that day. Perhaps he had already had enough of "following Hampton," and was thinking of the pleasures and comforts of home. He replied with some emphasis: "Can't make no fire to cook by in dis country, my Master; 'tis a miserable country, sah; dare ain't no light-'ood in it, sah."

It must here be explained that the lively flame from a few chips of fat resinous wood, known as light-wood, from the pitch pine of the coast-belt, is essential to the comfort and happiness, as well as to the facility of cooking, of the average low country Carolina darkey, and his estimate of another region is apt to be largely based upon the existence or the reverse of that to him indispensable commodity. A world without light-wood is indeed to him no world at all, but represents

> " The dismal situation, waste and wild,
> A dungeon horrible, on all sides round—
> Regions of sorrow, doleful shades, where peace
> And rest can never dwell, hope never comes,
> That comes to all."

At quite an early hour that morning (May 27th) Gen. Hampton rode up to regimental head-quarters, accompanied by two of his staff, one of whom was Captain Preston, known and loved by all his friends under the title of Jack Preston, with whom most of the Dragoons were acquainted. Gen. Hampton had just come from receiving his orders from Gen. Lee, and he now directed Col. Rutledge to proceed without delay in a direction to be shown by a courier left for the purpose. He was understood to say that there would be "real serious work" the next day.

The regiment was soon mounted, and marched across the South Anna River, passing the track of the Virginia Central Railroad, and then on towards Atlee's Station. On the route greetings were exchanged with several acquaintances from home who were met. The roads were much blocked by wagons in some places, and at one point Lieut.-Col. Stokes of the Fourth, impressed with the importance of avoiding delays, was endeavoring to clear the way for the passage of his column by announcing that he was ordered to "follow Hampton." One fellow was heard to mutter grimly in reply, "They'll soon have enough of following Hampton!" A halt for the night was made near Atlee's Station, Virginia Central Railroad. At that time brigades of infantry could be seen moving along the same road the Fourth had been traversing. The adjutant had occasion that evening to seek Gen. Hampton, and when on this errand learned from other sources that cavalry was supposed to be collected in the vicinity for an important demonstration to be made the next day.

Most of the cavalry of the army, with the exception of the newly arrived Division, were well uniformed in gray jackets, and were armed generally with breech-loading carbines captured from the enemy. The fresh Division just from the South was chiefly clad in "home-spun," a brown cloth unserviceable, and very unsoldierly in style, and they carried muzzle-loaders not quite as long as infantry rifles, which were awkward in appearance, and unwieldy for cavalry when mounted. So the old soldiers amused themselves with much good natured "chaff" at the expense of the new arrivals, and such remarks as "I say, Parson, let me have your long-shooter and I'll bite off the end," were very plentiful. The Army of Northern Virginia was largely composed of fellows who were sure to lay hold of everything that could be compelled to do duty as a joke, and if they did not "laugh and grow fat," their failure to do the latter was not their fault.

Shortly after sun-rise the next morning (May 28th), Captain Lowndes, an aide-de-camp of Gen. Hampton, and formerly a "Drag," rode up with the General's "compliments to Col. Rutledge," who asked him "to be kind enough" to order his regiment to mount and proceed with a courier, who would show him the road. Soon afterwards the Fourth was halted for a few minutes opposite to Hampton's head-quarters, in a piece of woods bordering on the road. There the General was seen standing near a little table, upon which were some papers. He was issuing his orders to his Brigade Commanders, as well as to Major-Gen. Fitzhugh Lee, who commanded a division, and was next

in rank in the cavalry to Hampton, whose commission was only
a few weeks older. Generals Rosser and Lomax were pointed
out to the new comers, and Dugue Ferguson of Fitz Lee's staff,
an "ex-Drag," was there, as also Major Barker and Taylor (the
latter also an "ex-Drag") of Hampton's. Cavendish, unmis-
takably an Englishman, who did gallant service under the Southern Cross, was observed too among the group near the General.

The regiment before long resumed its march in column of
fours, and Hampton and his staff galloped ahead. The road
being narrow the progress of the Fourth was rather slow, and
after proceeding about a mile and half the rattle of small arms
and now and then the booming of artillery, were heard. At
that all knew of course the affair had opened, and just then a
courier came galloping to Col. Rutledge with orders to hurry
forward his column. So the command rang out, "Trot! March!"
and it became almost at once not a "trot," but a good round
gallop. There were many there who were going under fire for
the first time, and oh! how their blood tingled as they dashed
forward. Prominent among their feelings was no doubt the
simple sense of duty, but in many and many a generous heart
there was more, far more than that; there was a spirit of self-
sacrifice, a burning desire to do, or die in emulation of some
favorite hero of history, or perhaps of romance, with an absence
of the sense of novelty in the sights and sounds, as if they awoke
instinctive memories from a remote past, inheritances of the
ever-warring Anglo-Saxon race, recurring

"Like glimpse of forgotten dreams."

After thus advancing at a rapid pace for about a mile and a
half, Butler's Brigade, which was used as a reserve, was halted
in an open space in column of regiments, the Fourth leading,
followed by a Georgia Battalion of nine companies, Dunnovant's
Regiment (5th S. C.) bringing up the rear, the 6th not having
as yet reported. Gen. Hampton was present giving orders, Col.
Rutledge being in command of the brigade, as Gen. Butler was
not on the field. This position was close behind the line of
battle, as was soon realized. It was there that a sight was witnessed some will never forget, for it was the first poor fellow
killed in battle they had ever seen. He was a Lieutenant who
was being brought out by two friends, his body lying on both

sides of his horse with the back against the saddle, the blood
pouring from the death-wound. He was a very fine specimen
of a man, over six feet in height, broad in proportion, long-
limbed and muscular. His unmilitary dress of homespun rendered the spectacle more pathetic, suggesting thoughts of a lov-
ing wife who had woven it: he looked to be and no doubt was
an American farmer dying in defence of his home, slain probably by a chance bullet fired by some of the foreign recruits
whom the North had bought by thousands at so much a head.
The ludicrous came close on the heels of the tragic, and perhaps
it was as well that this should have been the case. A courier
was sent to carry a message, and started on a gallop across the
open field. Hardly had he done so when a shell exploded near
him, a fragment striking his horse on the head and producing
death so quickly, that the poor animal rolled over almost as a
hare will do when killed running at speed. The courier turned
a somersault worthy of a first-class acrobat, but was not much
hurt. Getting on his feet in a somewhat dazed condition, the
man looked furtively first on one side and then on the other, as a
frightened rabbit might do before springing up, and then bolted
back in the direction from which he had ridden, with incredible swiftness, his sabre trailing out behind him almost horizontally. At the droll sight a hearty peal of laughter went up from
the brigade, such as must rarely have been heard before on a
battle-field.

The engagement then taking place is known as Hawes' Shop,
getting its title from a blacksmith of that name there located.
This fight and that which the cavalry fought on the next day
but one, are to be regarded as minor, but necessary links in the
chains of strategy which Lee's genius had forged to bar the road
to the capital of the Confederacy. It generally is the fate of a
cavalryman to die unheeded on some lonely picket-post, or to
fall unknown in a hand-to-hand struggle in a nameless skirmish,
but by great good fortune it was allotted to Butler's Brigade to
commence its career in Virginia amidst the historic actions of a
most brilliant campaign. Grant had begun on the 4th day
of that month of May, the movement by which he intended to
destroy Lee's army and capture Richmond. His force up to and
including Cold Harbor, was numerically, compared with that of
his adversary, about as 100 are to 40, besides large reserves

on which to draw. The Army of the Potomac was well disciplined and admirably equipped: it was handled well and fought hard, for Grant was able in tactics, the mechanical part of war, if deficient in strategy, the brain-work. His immense columns were hurled against the Army of Northern Virginia at the Wilderness, Spottsylvania Courthouse, and in minor battles, only to recoil shattered and bloody. Finally, at Cold Harbor on June 3d, after a brave fight in which thirteen thousand of his troops fell, twenty fold more than Lee's losses,* Grant abandoned the " Overland Campaign," and laid siege to Petersburg, in spite of his declaration that he would " fight it out on this line if it takes all summer." His losses during those thirty days were over sixty thousand against eighteen thousand Confederates: that is to say, he lost at least as many men as Lee had in his entire army.†

The Fourth was the first regiment of the brigade dismounted to fight at Hawes' Shop, Lieut.-Col. Stokes, a good man and true, commanding. It was the duty of each fourth trooper to hold the horses of three comrades who were to fight on foot. An amusing thing on such occasions was to watch how some fellows manœuvred to be " No. 4;" others, on the contrary, would exchange places if happening accidentally to occupy the " safe place," taking a pride in never serving as horse-holders. The Fourth mustered on this day 400 riders; when the 300 dismounted troopers came out from among the horses and formed, one was struck by the contrast in appearance, the formidable-looking body of horse having dwindled into an attenuated line, comparatively insignificant. Nine companies of the Fourth were ordered to take position on the right of the line then engaged, Co. K (the " Drags ") to be held in reserve after reaching a point designated. All started in good style, giving a splendid Confederate battle-yell, and the rifles of the rest of the regiment soon announced that they were making their debut as soldiers of the Army of Northern Virginia, while the Dragoons were proceeding to their appointed place through an open woods where the trees were far apart and without underbrush. Here Alexander Robertson fell, shot probably by a chance bullet. He was left in charge of two comrades to be put in an ambulance:

---

*Swinton's "Army of the Potomac," page 494.
†Swinton's "Army of the Potomac," page 491.

6

they soon rejoined their company, for their services could no longer avail the poor fellow. Reaching a point on the edge of the wood. the Dragoons were halted, and sat, or lay down, to avoid attracting unnecessary attention from sharp-shooters. Here they waited some little time: it was a silent party, for, like the Irishman's owl, they "did not talk much, but kept up a devil of a thinking." After a while orders came to take position on the right of the line with the second squadron, the first occupying the extreme right. First Lieutenant Lionel C. Nowell led the Dragoons, Capt. Colcock having been permanently invalided by service in malarial districts: Lieutenant O'Hear had been detailed for the day as acting adjutant to Lieut.-Colonel Stokes, with William Kirkland and Frank Middleton as couriers, Adjutant Manigault accompanying Col. Rutledge commanding the brigade. Lieutenant Harleston had been ordered the day before to Richmond to attend to procuring ordnance stores, and was therefore absent on this duty. It thus happened that Lieutenant Nowell was the only commissioned officer with the Dragoons. It was necessary to pass across an open piece of ground to reach the place to which they had been ordered. As they were doing this in single file. the attention of the enemy's sharp-shooters was attracted, and by their fire Percival Porcher was mortally wounded, and Tim O'Brien seriously hurt. Porcher fell across the path they were traversing, so that several of the men had to spring over his writhing body to proceed on their way. Soon the open space was passed, and another wood, with much thicker cover than the first, was entered, and then in a few seconds they were at it with a will. It is a difficult matter to describe properly a cavalry fight, because, as compared with infantry engagements, it is a rough-and-tumble affair, frequently carried on in thick cover, much in the Indian style. But it is only for the writer to relate incidents concerning the Dragoons, and to attempt nothing more.

On the left of their line, and parallel with it, ran an old drain-age ditch, or perhaps it was a rifle-pit used in some former campaign. Forward into this a considerable number of the men pressed, as it afforded a convenient protection from which to fight. and from there they soon began to make it hot for the enemy, many of whom were as close to them as thirty yards. The cover, as already mentioned, was thick, and the smoke soon

becoming entangled in this, made shooting at individuals difficult. Most of the shots had to be snaps, fired at faces only for
a second thrust from behind a tree, or peering round a bush, or
at the rifle flashes, which were sending the lead zipping and
singing through the air like devil's bumblebees. Then came in
play practice had by many a boy in the forests and fields of
Carolina with his rifle at the squirrels, or with gun among the
birds. A group of four Federals had crept up quite near, se-
curely concealed, as they thought, by a dense clump of bushes.
A "Drag" touched on the shoulder two of his nearest comrades,
and pointed with his finger. Three rifles deliberately aimed,
cracked, and there was then only one live man left behind that
bush. This one realized his shelter to be "a delusion and a
snare," but to reach a better would be compelled to expose himself still more, which he hesitated in doing. He, as well as she,
"who hesitates is lost," for when at length he made up his mind
to run the gauntlet, those three rifles had been reloaded and
cracked again, and "subsequent proceedings interested him no
more." Similar occurrences were taking place on the right of
the Dragoons' line, but there the trees were not numerous, and
the under-brush furnished poor protection, and it was in this
position that the first casualties happened. Would to God they
had possessed the breech-loaders which their foes were plying,
for then, besides the great advantage gained in rapidity of firing,
no exposure of the person in loading would have been required.
Here it was that Arthur Robinson was instantly killed, the same
bullet that passed through his head striking in the skull also
Jas. Adger, a bright lovable boy, and ultimately causing his death.
The two were great friends, and when Adger saw his mess-mate
fallen, in spite of his own painful disabling wound, he tried his
best to crawl to his assistance. Bedon, too, was killed. He had
a presentiment that he was to die that day, and when he dismounted for the fight had handed to his horse-holder, for safe
keeping, a miniature containing a fair girlish face, which until
then had hung around his neck.

Thus the fighting went on, and every moment the boys settled
down better and better to their work. Some have thought that
they unnecessarily exposed themselves, not sufficiently taking
advantage of the trees and other cover, and that to this was in
part due their large percentage of loss, but I think that is a mis-

take. Lieutenant Nowell, ever attentive to the well-being of his men, was constantly observing that their safety was not needlessly disregarded, and they fought as coolly and intelligently as one would expect from such stuff. After a time, how long in hours and minutes is impossible to compute in battle, it was observed that bullets came from the left of the Dragoons' line, and parallel with it; they had the peculiarly vicious whisper and screech that flanking shots always possess; an unmistakable and especial devilishness which is at once recognized. Lieutenant Nowell at first supposed the squadrons on his left to have become confused in their position in consequence of the thick cover, and that they were firing on their friends by mistake; therefore these flanking shots were not returned. In a few minutes Adjutant Jeffords of the Fifth rushed from the right, where he had been reconnoitering, and shouted to Nowell to get out of that position, as it was flanked on both sides. Stepping backward a few yards into a comparatively open space, Nowell could see that his company was being encircled from the left, and springing back to his men, ordered them to save themselves by a rush-out and through the circle. This they did, but in the flanking movement most of their casualties occurred, as in getting out of the position the gauntlet had to be run of many shots at close quarters. The retreat was made out of the wood and across the open field beyond, through which they had come to go into the fight. At the further side of the field was a rail fence, behind which they formed, throwing it down and using the rails as a breastwork. Here they waited in a perfectly orderly manner, again and again pealing their battle cry, expecting the approach of the enemy. To reach them he would have been compelled to try crossing the open field, which he would have found a different matter from hiding in the bushes. There were no Confederate troops in sight at that time, except the Dragoons formed behind the fence and some men from the regiment who had joined them. The enemy, however, only fired a few shots at long range from the edge of the woods, having imbibed apparently a good deal of respect for the "long shooters." Very soon Lieut.-Colonel Stokes, commanding the Fourth, rode up from the rear and ordered Nowell to withdraw his company to their horses. Thus ended the affair. It seems that two couriers had been sent to order the Fourth to withdraw from the fight, but the squadrons on the right failed to receive this command, and therefore were not aware that the companies on their left had been removed, and that the way was thus left open for their being surrounded.

The cavalry, when dismounted, were not usually accompanied into battle by their colour-bearers, because, as the fighting was chiefly done in woods, and from behind cover, it was not advisable to attract the enemy's attention to their position by the display of a flag. As the "Dragoons" returned to their horses, at the head of the Regiment floated the Southern Cross, and some of them will never forget the sensations it produced. Let a cold-blooded civilian in time of profound peace, comfortable, well-fed, secure, say, if he will, that a flag is a mere nothing; he knows no better. But nevertheless it can be a living breathing reality, vital with the principles it symbolizes, and thus it seemed to those boys that day coming with thinned ranks out of the fire, and smoke, and blood, and as such will it always be remembered.

When the men reached their horses, Sergeant Huger (Ben Huger) was missing. Some one had seen him coming wounded across the field towards the rail breast-work, but none remembered to have observed him at that place. So one of his messmates, leading his horse, rode back to find him, and met him not far from the rail fence. In the flanking movement he had been shot through one arm near the shoulder, but had managed to come out, and though much weakened by the wound, was plodding quietly and patiently along towards where he supposed the horses to be stationed, holding the disabled arm and his revolver with the uninjured hand, having been obliged to abandon the Enfield, much to his mortification. He greeted his friend in his charming manner, seeming to be much touched by the very trifling risk incurred on his behalf, although it was really nothing, and any one would have been glad to help him, for he was dear to all, old and young, saints and sinners. He did not wish to be relieved of his pistol, which he was carrying with difficulty, saying he would prefer to have it on his person in the field-hospital, as it might be useful for shooting a surgeon; he had a not uncommon notion that those gentlemen are often too prompt about amputations.

The fighting was over, but the saddest part remains to be told.

The Fourth had lost in killed and wounded over 80 out of 300 men carried into action. The two squadrons on the right had of course suffered most, but the losses of the Dragoons were the heaviest. Of the forty-seven rank and file which they had sent in, 10 were killed or mortally wounded, 8 more had been severely wounded, and one other had been made prisoner unhurt: this last was Evans, a mere boy, who had not long before joined the company, and as he remained a prisoner until the end of the war, this was his first and last experience of battle. Lieutenant O'Hear, who, as stated, was that day acting adjutant of the Fourth, had been surrounded by the enemy as he was endeavoring to extricate his men, and was killed while emptying among them all the chambers of his revolver. The day before he was noticed riding along in silence, with down-cast look and dejected air, very different from his usual manner, for he was in strong health and of a bright, joyous disposition: as good a fellow as ever lived. A friend asked him what "was troubling him;" at first he said, "nothing," but upon being further pressed on the subject, replied: "Well, I will tell you: I shall never see my wife, or South Carolina again." This, remember, was not the sickly depression of a dyspeptic, but proved the true presentiment of a brave man, who met expected death unflinchingly. Frank Middleton, who was acting as his courier, was pierced by three bullets, fell into the hands of the Federals, and died in hospital the next day. A Federal officer, who spoke to him there, was particularly impressed "with the quiet and composed manner in which he awaited death." Doubtless he lost his life in trying to reach his comrades on the right to warn them that they were being surrounded. Kirkland, one of the most amiable of men, also acting as O'Hear's courier, was mortally wounded, but was not made prisoner. Louis Vander Horst, loved by every member of the company, Allan Miles and Holmes, had all fallen. White (Billy White, as the "boys" called him), severely wounded, had fallen into the hands of the enemy in the flanking movement, and for the remainder of the war the camp-fires and marches of the "Drags" sadly missed his genial face, cheery voice and good stories.

This engagement at Hawes' Shop had lasted from about ten o'clock in the morning until nearly five P. M. It had resulted in unmasking and locating the enemy's infantry at a very critical period of the campaign, had inflicted severe losses upon his cavalry, which materially checked them for the future, and above all had convinced friend and foe that dismounted Confederate troopers would fight against vastly superior numbers with the stubborn tenacity of infantry, a fact which augured well for the success of Hampton's "new departure" in handling this branch of the service. It had also the effect, as far as the Fourth was concerned, of establishing a feeling of good-fellowship between the other companies and the "Dragoons," for before that the latter had been regarded with some jealousy, in consequence of being better dressed; there had been a touch of the "bloated bond holder" epidemic in fact, which was thus pretty nearly cured. After all, it seemed that "the might which slumbers in a peasant's arm," could be equalled, perhaps surpassed, by the spirit animating stalwart limbs and hard muscles in some other fellows. No more was heard from the regiment about that "kid-gloved company," and often delicate little compliments were paid (which might easily have been dispensed with) in yielding to the "Drags" particularly hot spots and lonely picket-posts.

It is not a little amusing, and at the same time very gratifying, to observe in several reports of this affair, made by Federal officers, how greatly they have exaggerated the size of Butler's Brigade, and how hard it hit. *One speaks of it as being composed "of seven large regiments (!) principally from South Carolina;" †another says the engagement was "the severest cavalry fighting of the war," and that "the enemy was a new brigade from South Carolina, and was very formidable." Custer says, referring to his own brigade, "Our loss was greater than in any other engagement of the campaign," and adds "We held our position here until after dark, when we were relieved by the infantry." Alger, of the 5th Michigan, speaks of "the enemy" offering "an obstinate resistance, fighting our men hand to hand;" and Gen. Davies reports the fight as "a very severe engagement, which lasted seven hours."

On the night of this 28th of May, the Fourth bivouacked about two miles to the rear of Hawes' Shop. On the way there

*Gen. Custer.
†Col. Kester, 1st New Jersey Cavalry, in report made to the *Governor* of his State.

they passed infantry going in the direction from which they had come; Gen. Breckenridge was in command, a fine looking officer. Before the men had dismounted Gen. Hampton rode up to inquire about the losses, having heard that they had been severe, especially in Co. K (the " Dragoons ").

The next day (Sunday, May 29th,) was spent by the regiment at the place at which they had camped the evening before, and many friends called upon the " Dragoons " to inquire about their losses, and to express sympathy. Large masses of infantry were on the move all day, and thus was afforded the opportunity of seeing on the march the veterans of the Army of Northern Virginia. Well might the new comers gaze with enthusiasm on the " incomparable infantry " of that army, distinctively American, which had recently won a series of victories worthy of " song and story." No wonder that their blood tingled and their young hearts throbbed as they looked, for since yesterday they could claim with these the brotherhood of comradeship. A tough-looking weather-beaten set of fellows they were, many not having changed their clothing for three weeks, but in spite of all that they had about them a cheerful jaunty devil-may-care air. The line-officers trudged along with their men, generally carrying as much weight, except for rifles, as the privates, and wearing uniforms almost as worn and stained. May our country have many another fine army in the years to come, but surely " ne'er shall we see *their* like again."

Occasionally there would be a halt in the passing columns, and opportunities would thus be given of exchanging a few words with some of the men. Most of them had heard of the severe fight sustained by the cavalry the day before, and frequently words of commendation and sympathy were kindly spoken, which, coming from these veterans, were very pleasant to hear. Many General Officers rode past, among others the famous Corps-Commander, A. P. Hill. To the backs of some of the head-quarter wagons would be haltered a milch cow, which was the only sign of " luxury " to be seen. The soldiers jokingly said these were for making milk-punches, but it is to be feared the other ingredients were lacking.

That day the " Dragoons " received rations of bacon and hard-tack drawn on their full roll of *the day before,* and as most of the negro servants had happily been sent back to the wagons, food for once was plentiful. By melting the fat of bacon in a frying-pan and steeping pieces of hard-tack in the boiling liquid, a dish was made which seemed then very savory, though the recollection of it now is suggestive of nightmare. The fellows were grouped together, mostly around one fire, messes being disorganized by the events of the previous day, and chatted among themselves like school boys. The scene is as fresh in the writer's memory as if it had occurred yesterday. There was Jimmy Bee, noted for his kindly generous disposition, traits which are far better shown in camp and on the march than in any other way: Charlie Prioleau was there, and Poinsett Pringle always bright and agreeable. The losses of the company were much discussed. Oliver Middleton was standing by the fire, watching wistfully with big honest boyish eyes the pieces of hard-tack fizzing in the frying-pans. He had the faculty of always looking neat, and his face wore a refined expression, which was very attractive. Like the others, he deplored the havoc wrought in their ranks the day before: "But," said he, "we came here to fight, and it is *our place to fight*, and *die*, if need be." The manly sentiment was in his mind of "*noblesse oblige*," although he was too unassuming to express it in that way.

On the next morning (May 30th), soon after sunrise, the brigade started on a march. Gen. Butler was in command, having arrived on Saturday evening. As the Sixth Regiment had by this time reported, the brigade was complete: on the march that day it was joined by the Rutledge Mounted Riflemen (two companies) and Gary's Battalion (eight companies): this combined force Butler was to handle, no other troops co-operating. Soon after the start two enterprising newspaper vendors were met. These "gentlemen of the press" were driving along comfortably in a buggy, looking as sleek and well-fed as possible. There seems to be no place in which one will not meet a newspaperman, unless it be in heaven or a battle. The march took the command through Mechanicsville, and then in the direction of Gaines' Mill, all historic, indeed "holy ground." Both places were disappointing in appearance to those who expected them to be in keeping with the great events of which they had been the scenes, the former consisting of only a small collection of dilapidated little houses. Having passed Gaines' Mill the march proceeded along the Old Church Road, when suddenly the prox-

7

imity of the enemy was demonstrated by two of his soldiers on foot being seen near a farm-house just off the road. These fellows made off at sight of the cavalry, which was at once ordered to the trot, and went forward for about half a mile further in the direction of Cold Harbor. None of the men had the least idea of what the programme was to be, and probably the line-officers were no wiser, but when a halt was made in a ploughed field on the left of the road, and some squadrons were dismounted to "feel the position of the enemy," they all knew they were " in for it " again.

Lieut.-Colonel Gary was placed in charge of the line of attack, and the force was ordered in by squadrons, as they were needed. The "Dragoons" were among the last remaining on their horses, but at length the order for them rang out, "Dismount to fight!" Most of these young fellows went into action that day with the irrepressible cheeriness and disregard of danger which belong to youth and courage, for they were privates, and therefore without the sense of responsibility which makes many a conscientious officer experience in such trying moments a sinking of the heart, even a sickness of the stomach, often mistaken for fear.

The "Dragoons" dismounted for the fight 28 men under the command of First Lieutenant Nowell. The horses, under the charge of the holders, as usual, were left near a road leading through a tract of woodland, and the company advanced through a field on the left, and took position behind a rail fence on the further side, which rested upon a road. The enemy was posted behind fences, whilst a farm-house and out-buildings in a field on the other side of the road also furnished them shelter. When the "Dragoons" got into position to open fire they found very hot work going on, which is not surprising, as the sequel will show. The fence, however, had been thrown down, and converted into a sort of temporary breastwork, and by lying down behind this partial protection, they did some effective shooting. It was here that Withers, a mere lad, not yet full grown, in standing up in haste to load, received a bullet through the crown of his felt hat, which cut some hair from his head without hurting the scalp. "Spoilt my hat," said he, taking off the injured article and looking at it somewhat ruefully, for a hat was valuable property in those days; "but I'll never again grumble at not being taller." Before long the bullets began to come from the left, and the fence ceased to be of much service as a protection; then every private knew, as well as if each had been the commanding general, that the line was flanked. Thicker and thicker came the bullets, and it looked as if every blade of grass and each weed in the field were being cut down as they skimmed past humming their devilish tunes. Soon after this a compact mass of blue extending rearward as far as one could see, was descried marching slowly down the road on the side of which the "Dragoons" were posted. The head of this column, when first observed, was 250 to 300 yards distant and was descending a slope or low hill. It was next to impossible for any one, however poor a shot, to fail of hitting that mass; so many stopped firing at the concealed enemy near them, and shot away as fast as possible into the advancing stream of blue, which was supposed to be the *infantry of the Army of the Potomac, and surely every bullet must then have had its "billet." But naturally this unequal contest could not be of long duration, and the troops posted to the right of the "Dragoons" were soon seen retreating, as best they could, and then Co. K was ordered back. But the coming out of this Hell was a terrible matter. Lieutenant Nowell on the left, counting his own life as nothing, was busied in endeavoring to extricate his men, who were fast falling around him, for by this time the enemy was sweeping the field with an overwhelming fire. And well might they sweep the field, for one Confederate Brigade was fighting a heavy body of Sheridan's Cavalry, supported by the extreme left of Grant's Infantry. It was only the boldness of the attack that prevented the affair from being ended much sooner, for the Federals advanced cautiously, supposing they were about to encounter infantry in force. Nowell was surrounded by a score of the enemy on whom he was firing his revolver, when struck in the waist by a bullet, only his sword-belt preventing the wound from proving fatal, and he was made prisoner. The "Drags," who managed to reach their horses, were only enabled to do so by the fortunate circumstance that a fringe of woodland projected into the left of the open field, and afforded them some slight cover in retreating. A sad number from their ranks were lost that afternoon. Poor Jimmy Bee no more would ride the pretty petted mare he loved so well, for he was mortally wounded in traversing the wood-edge, and

---

*Gen. Custer's Report states that no infantry was actually engaged.

Adams was shot while giving him assistance. Poinsett Pringle's handsome face, lithe athletic figure and winning manners would never again attract man or please the eyes of woman, and Charlie Prioleau had gone down near the rail fence. Oliver Middleton, fighting like a hero on the left, hemmed in by foes, had laid down his young life for his country; a boy in years, but his charming face and manly bearing gave assurance of a useful and gracious maturity. The New South, with all its boasted material progress, possesses no treasures so precious as those that the Old South has buried. The other losses of the "Dragoons" consisted of two wounded and five others, besides Lieutenant Nowell, wounded and captured; these latter remaining prisoners until the end of the war. If you would appreciate what their sufferings in captivity must have been, read accounts emanating from Northern sources of the miseries represented as endured by their men in Libby and other Southern prisons; look over the descriptions of Andersonville, and examine carefully the pictures published by the New York *Tribune*, said to be fac-similes of some of the "victims:" when you have done all this, and thus wrought yourself up to the proper pitch of horror and commiseration, remember that, as appears from the *Official Reports of Secretary of War Staunton, and Surgeon-General Barnes, the death rate among Confederates confined in Northern prisons was over 12 per cent., and among Federal prisoners at the South less than 8½ per cent.; in other words, that one out of eight Confederates died, and only one out of twelve Federals, or proportionately three Confederates to two Federals, a difference of thirty-three per cent. in relative mortality. This was no doubt the result of Staunton's system of silent prison tactics. By stopping the exchange of prisoners customary between civilized combatants, he prevented the Confederacy from regaining the services of soldiers worth relatively three times their number of Union levies, and by establishing a suitable course of prison treatment, he ensured the least practicable quantity of Confederates being returnable, if the clamors of the relatives of Federal captives should force the administration to resume exchanges. At the South motives of an exactly opposite nature were stimulating the natural humanity of the authorities to take the best care possible under the circumstances of their prisoners, so as to have them in a condition to exchange when the earnestly hoped-for renewal of that practice should be obtained.

Thus the casualties in the "Dragoons" had amounted to 12 out of 28 carried into battle, and they lost the services of another man just after mounting. Edward Trenholm, who happened to have been horse-holder at Hawes' Shop, and in this fight, rode a very poor animal with quite a knack for falling down, which was exemplified on this occasion by his rolling over and crushing his rider so badly, that the latter was sent to hospital, and performed no more duty during the war.

After the troopers of the brigade had remounted their horses, they withdrew generally towards the rear much more expeditiously than was deemed advisable, as the enemy were exhibiting a disposition to push their pickets forward. Col. Gary called for volunteers to go back to check the Federals, to which the "Dragoons" responded at once with a cheer. This proceeding was not, however, carried out, but a rear-guard was formed consisting of the "Dragoons" and about two dozen men from the 4th and the other regiments, this detachment being under the command of Col. Rutledge. The retreat was then effected without any further losses, and without experiencing material molestation.

This affair of May 30th was called among the cavalry Cold Harbor, but it in fact took place about one and a half miles from that spot, at Matadequin Creek, and was fought four days before the great battle of Cold Harbor, which put an end to Grant's Overland Campaign against Richmond. The object of the movement was to ascertain in which direction Grant was advancing to attack, and this necessary information was thus gained. To put men into action boldly, and to extricate them at the proper moment, are the requisites in such feeling-operations, but the satisfactory accomplishment of this programme sometimes becomes difficult.

The brigade had gone into action soon after two o'clock, and had withdrawn about four. The enemy gave indications before sunset of being engaged in cautiously pushing forward their pickets in dangerous proximity to the Confederate lines. It was necessary, therefore, to send out a detachment to ascertain their whereabouts, and to picket the main road. A few of the "Dra-

goons " were ordered to lead to the rear the riderless horses belonging to their fallen comrades, and the rest, about ten in number, were detailed for the picket, which consisted in all of thirty
to forty men made up from various commands. The company
was now without commissioned officers, its first sergeant, Beckley, was ill, and second sergeant, Huger, wounded. The picket
detachment was placed under the direction of an infantry officer, because he was thought to be well acquainted with the roads
of that locality, and it proceeded carefully in the direction of
the enemy. The men had had nothing to eat since sunrise, and
not too much then; so in lieu of an evening meal they had to
take-up the buckle of their sword-belts several holes, like Dugald
Dalgetty, when similarly situated. The "Dragoons" were
placed in about the centre of the squad, instead of being
used as an advance-guard, as should have been done, when
the adventures of the evening would no doubt have termi-
nated differently. It was a clear summer night, but without
any light from the moon, and it soon became quite dark, especially under the shadows of the trees along the road-side and in
strips of woodland. Between nine and ten o'clock the picket
had worked its way slowly to a point on the road on the further
side of a small brook, where the ground rose slightly. Some six
or eight men, not belonging to Butler's Brigade, had been sent
ahead as an advance-guard. Just here the clatter of their
horses' hoofs returning at full speed was heard, and at once all
the other animals became very excited, snorting and pushing
against each other, and striving to turn round singly, disregard-
ing the formation of fours, a very unusual thing for them to do,
for their habit is to sidle together. Whether the advance-guard
was in panic-stricken flight, or whether it ran into the head of
the column because unaware of its proximity in time to draw
rein, is uncertain, but the effect was the same, whatever the
reason; there was a frightful collision in the darkness. At the
same moment a few rifles flashed in the men's faces fired from
the concealment of the fence and bushes on the road-side. Then
ensued a scene that baffles description. The column was in formation of fours, occupying nearly the entire width of the narrow road, on both sides of which were rather high and substantial fences. The horses became perfectly frantic with terror,
and each for himself strove madly to break through and get

away, and no doubt many of their riders were for the time being
as demoralized as the animals. It is not surprising that cavalry
are, on the average, much more liable to panics than infantry:
the cause is not far to seek. The excitement of the horse in-
creases that of the man, and vice versa, until both sometimes
become mere frantic brutes. The handful of "Dragoons," occupying nearly the centre of the column, endeavored to preserve
their formation and thus resist the pressure, but they were ridden down to a man. One, not seriously injured, managed, he
knows not how, to scramble and crawl from under the horses,
and found himself in a dark fence-corner among some black-
berry bushes and weeds. His rifle was lost, and his sabre, being
attached to the saddle, was also gone, but he drew his revolver
and lay quiet, hoping that in the darkness he would find an opportunity of escaping, for he supposed himself surrounded by
the enemy. Just behind where the "Dragoons" had been in
the column, the clay-hill had been trenched on the road-side by
the rains of many years into a ditch four or five feet in width
at the top, gradually narrowing to only a foot or two at the bottom, and eight feet or more deep. A better trap could hardly
have been devised for this particular occasion. Many horses
and riders had been pushed into this place, in several cases the
men being underneath: the cries for help and groans, and the
fearful shrieks of one broken-backed animal, are vividly remembered. People soon began moving about assisting sufferers and
clearing up the debris; in doing so often passing close to the
"Dragoon," who at length gradually realized that they were
friends, and came out from his hiding place. It was a frightful scene, for the poor victims pulled out from beneath the
horses, were literally covered from head to foot with blood, so
that they could not have been recognized by their own brothers.
The "Dragoons" lost their horses, some of which were never
recovered, and all their trappings and effects. One of their
men, Phillips, was crippled for life, and another, Howell, wan-
dering about in the darkness, fell into the hands of the enemy.
The others were more or less hurt, but not permanently disabled. The "Dragoon" already referred to assisted in getting
some of the wounded into a little farm-house, which happened
to be close at hand. Though by no means "on pleasure bent,"
"he had a frugal mind," and succeeded in procuring there a

small piece of corn-bread. The poor woman who gave it to him would accept no pay, although doubtless herself far from well-provided, but with sincere gratitude he took the food, reserving it to be eaten as soon as he had leisure for the purpose. Proceeding down the road a couple of miles in search of his horse, he met Julius Pringle doing the same thing, and on meeting neither could help laughing at the sorry appearance cut by the other. With bruised, dirty faces, torn clothes and without hats, the couple were certainly very unlike the idea given in fiction of the "dashing Dragoon." It reminds one of the incident related by Lieutenant Harleston as happening to him one night not long afterwards, during a picket on the Chickahominy. Weary and hungry, worn-out with fighting mosquitoes and breathing malaria, he and another young officer had been sitting together on a log without a word having been exchanged between them for an hour, when suddenly his companion raised his head and said: "Have you ever read Charles O'Malley?" Harleston, in some surprise, replied that he had. "It's a pack of lies from beginning to end!" exclaimed the other indignantly slapping his leg with his hand. Pringle and his companion felt somewhat in the same disgusted state of mind, but sought out a quiet nook in a wood near a wagon-train, divided the piece of corn-bread, smoked a pipe, and then slept as soundly until day-light as if there were no such things as "wars and rumors of wars," and soon after awaking succeeded in rejoining the company.

The next morning the "Dragoons," with the rest of the brigade, marched towards the Chickahominy, and remained for a day near Bottom's Bridge. A demonstration was made by the enemy, as if to cross the stream, but nothing came of it, except some disagreeable picketing at night with the Federals in front, and (what was worse) countless hordes of mosquitoes on all sides. It was here, however, that an event occurred, which to some of the "Dragoons" will always be more memorable than a hard fought battle, for they saw for the first time their preeminent commander, Lee. He was driven along a part of the picket-line sitting in a covered "Jersey wagon," and at one point stopped for a few minutes. No doubt he was reconnoitring personally the enemy's position, and discovered at a glance the feint at an attempted crossing of the river, which was then being made; the fruits of his study were soon to be conspicuous at Cold Harbor. At that time, as is now known, the General was far from well, the enormous strain of the previous thirty days having told even on his grand physique; this probably accounts for his not being then mounted on "Traveller."

The command moved from the river towards White Oak Swamp, and encamped at Frazier's Farm, a place rendered famous by the desperate stand there made by McClellan two years previously. Here, as elsewhere along his route, the hurried nature of McClellan's retreat was evidenced by the debris still visible: rusty canteens, cartridge-boxes and other leather accoutrements, now partially decayed: pieces of uniforms and blankets discolored by long exposure to the weather; fragments of rubber-cloths and similar reminders were strewed plentifully along the roads. It was easy to understand how rich the pickings must have been at the time, and to appreciate the customary generosity of the enemy in furnishing gratis Quartermaster's stores to Lee's army. Two days were spent at Frazier's Farm, and while the brigade occupied that position the great battle of Cold Harbor was fought, in which it did not participate, the fighting being confined to infantry and artillery. On that day (June 3d) one of the "Dragoons" was sent to search for his horse lost in the stampede of the night of May 30th, as the animal was supposed to be in the possession of some of the other Cavalry Brigades. It so happened that this trooper was not very far in the rear of the Confederate line engaged on that memorable day. The thunder of the artillery was indescribably grand. When the Federal charges were made, the guns from both sides would open in one continuous roar, like line-of-battle musketry, it being impossible to distinguish between the separate discharges, and when each time the attacking columns were repulsed, the awful roar would cease, and there would ensue a short interval of comparative quiet. It was thus possible to know by the ears, as well as if one witnessed it with the eyes, when Grant again and again ordered his troops to advance, and when they came again and again rushing back from the fruitless slaughter. Important results were being wrought during those minutes, while the "Dragoon" was listening to the terrible thunder, for Grant's "Overland Campaign" was then being ended amidst the carnage of thousands of his followers. But a a more momentous issue was well nigh reached. For at last a

general assault all along the line was ordered by Grant, but the
soldiers silently and sullenly refused to move forward;* then
their leader, if a man of a sensitive nature, stung to the quick
by the useless destruction of the flower of his army, and by this
proof of their broken spirit, would probably have sprung upon
his horse, called upon his troops not to *go*, but *follow*, and would
have carried Lee's position, or fallen in the heroic attempt. If
Grant had done so; if he had thus hurled in desperation his
massed columns upon the Army of Northern Virginia, they certainly would have dissolved into nothingness, like ocean-waves
dashed against granite cliffs, and the Army of the Potomac
would have forever ceased to exist. For such a catastrophe,
falling at that time upon the North, already "sick unto death"
of war, would have rendered it impracticable for the Federal
administration to recruit another army. If! Yes, but *if* eleven
months before, Longstreet had promptly obeyed Lee's orders,
Gettysburg, instead of a drawn battle, would have been a decisive victory, and the Confederacy now one of the nations of the
world. But let us not, overwise after "accomplished facts,"
talk flippantly of "ifs," for the result many times during those
four years was within a hair's breadth of the grasp. It is well
to remember this in these days when they would have us believe
that there never was a possibility of success for the side weaker
in numbers, as if the brightest pages of history were not illu-
mined by the victories of energetic devoted minorities.

Butler's Brigade was in bivouac at Frazier's Farm when orders
were received for an immediate march to Mechanicsville. The
"Dragoons" now numbered about a dozen men under the command of a non-commissioned officer. On the march the Fourth
passed along the rear of Lee's lines, and thus saw many a comfortable tent and ration-wagon and fat horse of the Quarter-
masters. It thus happened that the Major, who was Quartermaster of McGowan's Brigade, was met by Colonel Rutledge and
Adjutant Manigault, and they rode along together for a while
chatting. The Major had held the position but a few months,
and had desired about a year before this time to join the "Dragoons" as a private, the company then being stationed at Green
Pond, S. C., and "in clover." He had been dissuaded from doing
so, and must have been more than human if he did not now con-

*Swinton's "Army of the Potomac," page 487.

gratulate himself upon this, when the scant battered remnant of the once full and brilliant company was pointed out to him as it marched along to encounter further boiling-down in the cauldron of war.

In the afternoon Mechanicsville was reached, and there the night was spent. This place, like all old camping-grounds, was well stocked with that insect which has a special fondness for lean soldiers, familiarly known in those days as "I. F. W." ("in for the war"). On first acquaintance he was sickening, and his memory is unsavory; so let us mention him no more. There was much interested discussion and speculation that evening as to where the command was about to move, for it was understood that it was to march early the next morning, and five days' rations had been issued. Certainly a raid, or expedition of some kind was intended, but neither officers nor men had the slightest idea of where they were going. Change is usually welcome, and the mystery added a charm to the expected movement. Some said they were going to Washington; others perhaps looked forward to dancing in Baltimore, but no one doubted that there would be, at all events, plenty of "music" of a certain kind.

Early on the following morning the brigade was put on the march, proceeding north of Richmond. A steady walk was kept up all day, and when a halt for the night was ordered, some thirty miles had been made. The next morning the march was resumed. At about noon a short halt was made, and Gen. Butler then sent the Adjutant of the Fourth to say to one of the "Dragoons," whose horse had become slightly lame, that he was to quietly fall out of ranks, and return to the Reserve Camp near Mechanicsville, where unserviceable animals and men had been left. This incident was thought to indicate a long expedition, but at that time the Brigade Commander himself was not aware of his destination. It was not until the halt at night, about three miles from Trevylian Station, that he knew the object of the movement was to intercept Sheridan. This news soon became known among the men, and few of them will ever forget the occasion; the quiet summer evening, the cool crisp air, so grateful after the heat and well-nigh unendurable dust of the two days' march, and the blue mountain-ridges in the distance looking peaceful and pretty, and refreshing to the eyes.

The mention of the battle of Trevylian awakens lively sensations in the breasts of cavalrymen, and may well warm the hearts of all true men. Not only was it an affair on the result of which very important consequences depended, but it was probably the largest engagement in respect to numbers, and the most fiercely contested on both sides, of any cavalry encounter during the war. For it was exclusively a cavalry-battle, Sheridan having ventured to leave his infantry supports. On that field Hampton and the most dashing of the Northern horsemen confronted each other face to face, and there was demonstrated the relative merits of the combatants. For all these reasons the subject possesses especial interest, but it deserves lasting remembrance on even better grounds; for there was refuted the degrading sophistry that soldiers are only effective in proportion to their numbers, men differing inherently no more than grains of sand on the seashore. Federal accounts of this affair are, for obvious reasons, very meagre, and the little thus told does not always leave correct impressions. For instance, Sheridan said that he drove Hampton from the field, and pursued him until he "took refuge behind strong fortifications and heavy infantry supports at Gordonsville." In point of fact the "driving" was in the opposite direction; there were no fortifications nor infantry at Gordonsville, and the nearest approach to that place made by Sheridan was at Trevylian, twelve miles distant. Let us suppose that his errors are due to lack of appreciation of the difference in meaning between an active and passive verb, to defective eyesight in mistaking distant mountains for earth-works, and Hampton's "long-shooters" for serried ranks of foot-soldiers, and to imperfect knowledge of geography; but still it must be admitted that the historian in search of accuracy had better obtain his facts from sources more reliable than such official reports. From a Confederate stand-point the story of this battle has, for some reason or other, never been written, as far as I am aware.

On June 8th it had been ascertained that Sheridan had crossed the Pamunkey with a heavy force of cavalry and artillery. His objects were to destroy Gordonsville and Charlottesville, and to form a junction with Hunter, then in front of Lynchburg. After the capture of the latter place, Kautz would naturally have joined the combined force. The Federals would then be occupying a position that would strategically compel Lee to detach infantry to expel them, the necessity for which at this critical juncture might have caused the abandonment of Petersburg, upon whose lines Grant was rushing. The duel between Hampton and Sheridan consequently involved issues of such deep moment, that this cavalry encounter may well be considered unique in the history of the war. To frustrate the designs of Sheridan's expedition, Gen. Hampton followed him, taking for this purpose his own division and that of Major-General Fitz Hugh Lee, with artillery pertaining to these commands. The relative numbers of the opposing forces will be best understood by reference to the following extract from a report made after the war by Gen. Hampton to Gen. Lee:

"At that engagement my Division was about 2,800 strong, certainly not over 3,000, and Lee had present but 1,700 men. The troops engaged on our side did not therefore exceed 4,700 men, and were probably not more than 4,500. Among the papers captured during the fight were the field-returns of some of Sheridan's Brigades, and one paper gives the organization of his whole Corps. In the field-return of Custer's Brigade for May 31st, there were 'effective mounted men present for duty 1,484.' There were four regiments in this brigade, giving them an average of 371 men to each regiment. Sheridan had twenty-four regiments engaged in the fight, and putting each at the same average, his force amounted to 8,904 men."

At the War-Records Office at Washington there are *no returns of June 10th, 1864, for Sheridan's force, but a careful perusal of the official copies of the reports of his †Generals there to be found, must, I think, convince the reader that Hampton's estimate of his adversary's strength is not excessive.

From the above it will be seen that Sheridan had, in round numbers, two men to Hampton's one. Besides this, the Federals were armed with breech-loaders, and Hampton's Division, upon whom the brunt of the fighting fell, used muzzle-loaders. Moreover, Sheridan had picked men, the flower of Grant's Cavalry. There was that famous regiment, the " *Second,*" *corps d'élite* of the " Old Army." It had been organized in 1855, with Albert Sidney Johnston as Colonel, afterwards the hero, whom many rank in ability the third among Confederate commanders, and whose death at Shiloh, after he had reduced Grant's army to a mass of fugitives, they think a calamity second only to that of Stonewall Jackson; the Lieutenant-Colonel had been Lee, "A being apart and superior to all others in every way;—that towered far above all men on either side in that struggle:—the great American of the Nineteenth Century."* Hardee, Van Dorn, Kirby Smith, Hood, Fields, Major, Fitz Hugh Lee, men of note on the Southern side, and Thomas, Johnson, Palmer and Stoneman on the Northern, had been officers in this regiment. Then there were the First and Fifth Regulars, and Custer's Brigade, and some New Jersey Regiments, which were rated high, and other crack bodies. The artillery had also been carefully selected, and was in excellent order, the batteries having recently been reduced from six to four guns each. There were six complete batteries, aggregating† twenty-four pieces, whilst the guns on the Confederate side numbered only ‡twelve, or one to two of their adversaries.

Divining Sheridan's intentions, Hampton had succeeded in interposing his command on the night of June 10th, between the enemy and Gordonsville, thus covering that place and Charlottesville. During the night scouts brought in the intelligence that Sheridan had crossed the North Anna at Carpenter's Ford. He was entirely unaware that Hampton was in the neighborhood, and in quest of him, and had incautiously placed behind himself a river, supposing that he would have an undisputed march. He had " reckoned without his host," but so completely was he in the dark about Hampton's movements, that when his advance guard came into collision the next morning with the Confederate force, he mistook the latter for some local militia endeavoring to protect their homes.§

---

*Lord Wolseley, McMillan's Magazine, March, 1887.

†Information obtained from the Federal General J. M. Robertson, at that time stationed at White House, who was attending to business connected with the organization of the batteries with four guns instead of six.

‡Information obtained from Major Hart of Hart's Battery. The batteries were Hart's, Breathed's and Thomson's, of four guns each.

§Capt. Manigault, Adjutant of the Fourth, who fell into the hands of the enemy in the early morning of June 11th, learned this fact from conversations with Federal officers. Also see Gen. Torbert's Report.

Hampton at once realized the opportunity thus afforded him by his foe, and prepared to utilize it with his usual vigor. The moment had come not merely for checking his adversary, but for absolutely destroying him: surprised and driven back upon the river, his entire force would be devoted to ruin. The plan of the battle the writer believes was this:

In the morning at dawn Butler's and Young's Brigades of Hampton's Division would encounter the enemy advancing on the road leading from Clayton's Store (near the river) to Trevylian Station, on the (then styled) Virginia Central Railroad, whilst to the other brigade, Rosser's, was assigned the duty of covering a road on the left, branching from Clayton's Store, and leading towards Gordonsville. Fitz Hugh Lee's Division, camped that night near Louisa Court House, was ordered to move promptly to the attack down a road leading from that point to Clayton's Store, his left flank and Hampton's right thus mutually covering each other. This disposition was intended to place the two divisions united at Clayton's Store, Hampton driving the enemy in front, Fitz Hugh Lee flanking him on his left, and Rosser advancing to press his right flank, whilst the river blocked retreat. Then, it could be reasonably expected, would be dealt the *coup-de-grace* to Sheridan's host. The plan was simple, and admirable; why it was not *completely* successful will appear from the events to be related.

The air was chilly, the sweet-scented clover dripping with dew, and a bracing breeze coming from the dark mountain ridges, as the cavalrymen mounted in the first grey light of that June morning. A small piece of musty corn-bread hastily munched represented the only available substitute for breakfast, and some of the " Dragoons " had not even that, their negroes left at camp having retained the major part of the rations for five days there issued. Happy then would have been that mythical personage, who, it is said, " would rather fight than eat," but he would have mustered very few disciples among all those fellows with empty stomachs. However, there was soon something else besides hunger to think of, for the programme was commenced by a mounted charge of a squadron from the Fourth, which brushed aside a Federal* picket from the road

*It appears to have been from the Second Regulars (Lee-Johnston Regiment formerly).

leading to Clayton's Store, and then the brigade was dismounted and deployed on both sides of the road. Advancing a little distance the enemy was encountered, and the firing became quite brisk. The "Dragoons" (what was left of them, some twelve men,) went into action under the command of Lieutenant Cordes, who was assigned to that duty from one of the other companies of the regiment. He was a good officer, and much liked, but he was allowed scant time for enjoying the honor of leading the crack company of the Brigade, for he was soon wounded, and then the "Dragoons" were in their normal condition again, without a commissioned officer. Lieut. Harleston, who, as has been said, had been detailed for temporary service in attending to ordnance at Richmond, had hastened to rejoin his company, but did not succeed in accomplishing this that morning.

Butler's and Young's Brigades were performing the part allotted to them on the centre of the line; the enemy was being pressed back. Here Thomas Lining was killed, and better fellow never wore the "Dragoons'" uniform. He was colour-bearer of the Fourth, but, as already explained, it was not considered advisable to carry the flag in fighting on foot in a wooded country; during the actions at Hawes' Shop and Cold Harbor he had chafed very much at being compelled to remain with the horses, and he told the writer on the march to Trevylian, that he could not endure again such a position, and had arranged to carry a rifle and go with his old company into their next fight. So on this morning he had exchanged places with an ill man, taking his rifle and cartridge-box and falling-in with the "Dragoons." He was shot through the femoral artery, and died before assistance could be rendered. About this time also Wells was disabled by a bullet.

Rosser, too, was carrying out his instructions, so that on the left, as well as centre, everything was progressing satisfactorily. Surprised, and struck in an awkward situation, Sheridan was being hemmed in for destruction.

But suddenly the startling news came that the enemy in force was in the rear of the Confederate position, having passed round the right flank of Hampton's Division, which was not covered, as had been expected, by Fitz Hugh Lee's Division: the cause of this is unknown to the writer, but such was the fact. This changed of course the whole situation, and necessitated an instant alteration of the plan of battle. There was no time for *thinking* either; *action*, and quick as lightning, was required to save the Division from utter demolition. Rosser was therefore ordered by Hampton to dash from his position on the left, and charge the enemy then in the road behind the Confederate line of battle. This vigilant officer had already perceived that something was wrong, for he had noticed an immense cloud of dust rising to the skies from the place where the horse-holders of Butler's Brigade had been left. He immediately put his command into a gallop, and promptly struck the enemy, which proved to be Custer's Brigade. This latter corps was at that time occupying a road near the Railroad Track, and had captured some led horses, a few wagons, and three caissons. It was here that Burgess Gordon of the "Dragoons," being a horse-holder, fell into their hands. Rosser, with sabres and revolvers, made short work of Custer; taking from him his captures, besides making nearly an entire regiment prisoners, and driving most of the rest back as fugitives upon Fitz Hugh Lee, who, in consequence, bagged four caissons, and Custer's head-quarter wagon. It was necessary afterwards to read the papers found in the latter, in hopes of discovering some military information which might prove of value; in doing this, racy female correspondence came to light, but we will not "tell tales out of school."

As large numbers of dismounted cavalry had by this time pressed on to support Custer, it became necessary for the Confederates to move back in order to take up another line and form a junction with Fitz Lee. In carrying out this purpose Colonel Rutledge with the Fourth, was ordered to reverse the position of his regiment so as to check the enemy in their rear. It was then that Boone of the "Dragoons" was killed, a fine athletic youth, bold as a lion, merry as a lark, always "the life" of the camp; he died, no doubt, with a smile on his face, as a brave man should. Fairly, too, went down; he was acting as a courier that day, and lost his life while gallantly riding along the line in the face of a hot fire, carrying an order from the commanding officer. In fact the hostile lines were at that moment so near together, that he must have known the chances were greatly against his coming back alive, but nevertheless he did

9

his duty unflinchingly. Rutledge found the enemy in overwhelming numbers on the railroad, but managed by good judgment to keep his regiment interposed between the Federals and the rest of Butler's Brigade, until he succeeded, by moving some distance to his right, in taking position on the new line, which was successfully established near Trevylian Station by Hampton. Attempts were made by Sheridan to dislodge Hampton's Division from this place, but they were fruitless, both sides occupying their ground that night.

Sunday morning found the opposing forces holding the same relative positions, but by midday Fitz Lee had formed a junction with Hampton's Division, and was assigned a place from which he was to support the latter in case of an attack.

The brilliant military ability displayed by Hampton on Saturday, in extricating his command from a fearfully perilous situation, produced by no fault of his, should make this day memorable for all time. It was an occasion, too, on which his personal heroism, and the extraordinary influence exercised over his soldiers, marked him as the born warrior.

The position now occupied was, as has been stated, near Trevylian Station, on the (then styled) Virginia Central Railroad (now Chesapeake and Ohio Railroad), covering the wagon-road and other approaches to Gordonsville. To carry out the purposes of his expedition, it was necessary for Sheridan to proceed in that direction, but Hampton's "carriage stopped the way."

Quiet reigned during that Sunday morning, but it was the silence attending earnest preparation for effort on one side, and resolute unyielding determination on the other. At about three o'clock in the afternoon, Colonel Rutledge of the Fourth, was sitting on the top of a pile of wood by the railroad track, when the crack of a sharp-shooter's rifle was heard in the distance, and after an interval a bullet struck one of the logs with a thud. Gen. Butler, standing near, remarked, "That is the opening of the ball." And so it was.

Butler's Brigade occupied the left of the line, and the General now ordered Col. Rutledge of the Fourth to proceed further in that direction, so as more effectually to hold the point where the main road crossed the railway through a broad cut in the embankment. Most of the Fifth and the Sixth Regiments were on the right of the Fourth, and were posted chiefly behind the railroad embankment, which served as a partial breastwork; but the Fourth had very little cover, except a rail fence along the wagon-road, before it reached the railroad crossing. The brigade line thus formed was not straight, the Fourth and a detachment from the Fifth on its left, holding the critical point at the cut in the embankment, and extending thence to the left along the road at an angle.

Sheridan "meant business," as he soon showed. His dismounted regiments charged with energy the positions held by Butler's Brigade and the Fourth Regiment, with the detachment from the Fifth, was so placed that these necessarily sustained the heaviest part of the onsets. While they were in progress, Fitz Lee, by Hampton's orders, reinforced the left of Butler by Wickham's Brigade, which was posted behind the railroad embankment, and took the rest of his division, by a detour to the left, to strike the Federals on their right flank. Six charges were made by the enemy, and all had been repulsed. After each, however, the foe had retired to a lesser distance, so that after his sixth unsuccessful attempt to carry the position, he was established at perilously close proximity to the Confederate line, in some places only a few yards distant. Moreover he had managed to put some sharp-shooters in a farm-house, from the upper windows of which they were able to shoot down with considerable effect. Worse still, six guns had been brought into position, and were partially enfilading the entire brigade line, but more completely the Fourth. These pieces were capitally served, and were doing severe execution, the shrapnell killing men lying down behind the rail-fence breast-work as if they were in an entirely open field, a very hard thing for any troops to endure steadily, without the prospect of relief. His artillery also silenced a Confederate battery supporting the line, and was in fact "having it all its own way." To add to the trying nature of the situation ammunition had run short: it had been necessary to collect cartridges from the bodies of the dead and wounded, and now a very insufficient number remained with any of the regiments with which to resist further assaults, and the Fourth had nearly empty boxes.

There was a lull, almost a complete cessation in the firing, except on the part of the artillery; the enemy was "girding up his loins" for another and a final charge. To each Federal private a dram of whiskey was served, and a plentiful supply of metallic shells for his breech-loader.

All this while the Confederate troopers were enduring the trying ordeal with patient resolution. One young officer, as unmindful of his own danger as if his skin were bullet-proof, was walking down the line of his company encouraging the men, who were lying behind what cover there was, to fortitude. He reminded them of mothers and wives, sisters and sweet-hearts, who at their homes in the "far South," in their venerable much loved churches, were at that very moment sending up to the Most High prayers for their safety. It was an effective form of eloquence, for he was a sincere and brave man. Others again arrived at an equally desirable mental condition for fighting, in saying, or thinking, " Let the beggars come on, and be damned!" It amounted to the same thing in the end, for all, saints and sinners, were ready to "face the music." It was promised you that the Cavalry under Hampton should inaugurate a style of fighting equal in stubborn tenacity, as well as dash, to that of the magnificent infantry of the Army of Northern Virginia: then and there was the promise fulfilled; then and there was the pledge kept before the face of God and man.

It was at this time that Major Hart, who was working his guns on the right of the line, received through Captain Jeffords an urgent message from Gen. Butler, requesting him to bring his battery as quickly as possible, to where the Fourth and Fifth were stationed. Hart took two of his guns, all that could be spared, and galloped to the point indicated. He found the Federal sharp-shooters in the farm-house were doing great damage, and to them he paid his first attentions. Dividing his detachments and thus manning two of the abandoned guns already mentioned, he concentrated the fire of these and his own with short-range fuses upon the house, and in less than one minute from the time the first piece opened, he had the building in flames, and the sharp-shooters skurrying out for their lives. Then turning to the Federal battery on the right of the house, he poured into it so rapid and accurate a fire, that it was driven away in between ten and fifteen minutes. The importance of this service, thus gallantly, promptly and efficiently performed, can readily be appreciated, and every one connected with the cavalry well

knows that on this and many a similar critical occasion Major
Hart proved himself indeed " the man for Galway."

At nearly the same moment at which Major Hart reached the
ground, as related, the sorely needed ammunition also arrived.
The wagon came rattling down the road with the mules on a full
run, the driver lashing and cracking his whip. He continued
at the same furious pace along the line in plain view of the enemy, a man in the rear of the wagon throwing out the packages,
which were instantly caught-up, and the contents quickly found
their way into the hungry cartridge-boxes. It was well done
for a *wagoner*, and now " Richard was himself again."

At this hour the setting sun was just above the mountain-
ramparts with which nature has guarded "the Valley," lighting
up the peaks with a blaze of glory, touching the lower ridges
with the soft dreamy colours of hope, the nearer foot-hills looking almost despairingly black by contrast. It is strange how
sights like this, witnessed at important moments in man's life,
will linger always in the memory. Before the sun should sink
behind the fair warders of "the Valley," was to be decided the
fate of Gordonsville, Charlottesville and Lynchburg, perhaps of
Richmond.

The enemy advanced in force " to finish up the job," to push
the Confederates out of their position by sheer weight of numbers. They concentrated on Butler's Brigade, special gate-
keeper of the road they wished to traverse, and the Fourth and
part of the Fifth, as holding the key, were markedly singled out
for attentions. One body marched straight for the cut in the
embankment; it moved with beautiful precision, in close order,
shoulder to shoulder, the rifles, Spencers or Winchesters, held
horizontally at the hip, and shooting continuously. On they
came, and a few steps in advance, on one side, strode the leader,
a large fine-looking man, apparently a gentleman, with top-
boots extending above his knees, and corduroy riding-trousers.
His right arm was bent holding his cocked revolver pointing
perpendicularly upwards at the " Ready!" and he counted time
to keep his troopers in regular step. He presented a fine mark,
but somehow no bullets, it seemed, could hit him, and when any
of his men dropped, the rest closed-up beautifully and marched
straight on. It was a handsome sight, always to be remembered, but not an agreeable one just at that moment. This

brave fellow had almost reached the rail breast-work, when suddenly he stopped; very slowly the right arm descended until the pistol grasped in the hand pointed to the earth; he made an effort as if striving to brace-up, and then all at once the legs gave way, and it collapsed upon the ground, an inert lifeless thing. Immediately his men broke and ran. Just at that moment one of Hart's shells exploded an ammunition wagon, or a limber-chest, which evidently threw the enemy into some confusion. At that, as if by an electric impulse common to them all, the whole Confederate line leaped to their feet, sprang over the temporary breast-work with an exultant yell, and charged. The foe was driven back in disorder pell-mell upon his reserves, and at the same time Fitz Lee was seen pushing steadily forward in an open space, doubling-up their right flank. Then the great big fiery-faced Sun, having staid so long to see the fight over, sank joyously from sight behind the black mountains, for the day was won; Hampton had by sheer skill and pluck wrenched victory from the bloody fangs which had well-nigh rent his vitals.

After that it was only a question with Sheridan how to get away, and with Hampton how to prevent him. Butler's Brigade continued to occupy their former line, and the enemy kept up an irregular skirmish to cover their retreat, but it amounted to little more than an affair of sharp-shooters, and by ten o'clock all was quiet on that part of the field. It was before the last charge was repulsed that Col. Rutledge of the Fourth, while standing at the outside of his regimental line, had the shoulder and upper part of the sleeve of his coat cut by a bullet. Supposing the incident to be caused by some accidental shot, he thought nothing of it, but shortly afterwards the breast of his coat was furrowed by another ball. This was also attributed to chance, but just then one of the officers of the regiment came up to speak to him, and had hardly commenced doing so when his cheek was scratched by a bullet, and soon afterwards another ploughed through his beard, tearing out a handful of hair. All these shots came from the same quarter, and it was therefore concluded were fired with "*malice prepense.*" Naturally people cannot be expected to like having their clothes torn, faces scratched, and beards plucked so unceremoniously; so two men apt at exhortation were quietly sent forward to find this rude fellow, and protest against such conduct. These crawled along cautiously in the proper direction, and were not long in espying their man: he was a big red-haired Celt, occupying a slight elevation on which was a tree, from behind which he was peering out with cocked rifle watching for another potshot, as if engaged in land-lord shooting. The two soldiers from the Fourth promptly served their protest, doing this simultaneously so as to leave an agreeable doubt as to which gave the settler, and down he sank all in a heap. The next morning they found this red-haired person of homicidal proclivities stiff and stark, with rifle full-cocked lying between his legs. "They who take the sword, shall perish by the sword," it is said, and we may suppose the same thing fairly applies to rifles.

The enemy availed himself of the darkness, and all that night was engaged in making good his escape. One of the "Dragoons," who had been wounded on Saturday morning and had been left at a farm-house, fell into the hands of the Federals during the evolutions preparatory to establishing the second Confederate line. This house was turned into a field-hospital by Sheridan's surgeons, and over the entire yard and some ground outside were lying the wounded and dying, with plenty of amputated legs and arms to match. The wounded prisoners were treated with humanity, but of course suffered much: however, roasting in the sun all day, and shivering with chattering teeth in a shower of rain on Saturday night, were compensated for by the tramping of thousands of hoofs on the road close by, as the enemy hurried past all Sunday night in full retreat, leaving behind their wounded in charge of one of their surgeons. It was at this field-hospital during Saturday and Sunday, that the "Dragoon" mentioned received many kindnesses from a Sergeant and Private of the celebrated "Second." Both of these spoke in the warmest terms of respectful regard of Albert Sidney Johnston, and to this feeling for him was probably due in a great measure their good nature towards the wounded Confederate. It was a rather singular coincidence, that this same "Dragoon," happening in the early part of 1862 to be at one of the Forts in New York Harbor, heard there a sergeant, a big stalwart fellow, say excitedly to a knot of his comrades, "I tell you Albert Sidney Johnston was the best man that ever walked on God's earth!"

The Dragoons had lost at Trevylian three killed: the officer

assigned to command them and one man were wounded, and one
(a horse-holder) was captured: a loss of fifty per cent. The
Fourth Regiment suffered severely, but to what numerical extent the writer does not know, as Adjutant Manigault fell into
the hands of the enemy in carrying a message on Saturday morning, when the opposing lines were only a few yards apart. The
total loss in Hampton's Division amounted to *612, of which
295 were missing; that in Fitz Lee's was very light. I have no
knowledge of a regular official report of his casualties in the
battle of Trevylian having been made by Sheridan, but he states
that he thinks those of his corps from May 4th to July 30th,
aggregated "between 5,000 and 6,000." A large percentage of
this punishment was inflicted at Trevylian, *977 prisoners (including 125 wounded) having been taken from him in that battle, and during his retreat to the cover of the gunboats, and his
killed and wounded were certainly correspondingly heavy.

On Monday Hampton pressed on in pursuit of the foe, who,
having "head-start," succeeded in crossing the North Anna at
Carpenter's Ford. As Sheridan was provided with a pontoon-
train, which enabled him to cross rivers at any point, and as the
Confederate force had none, it was necessary for the latter to
remain on the Southern sides of the streams, so as to keep between him and Grant's army, and thus prevent the junction,
which he was trying to effect. For several days the hostile columns thus marched on parallel lines, the enemy carefully avoiding a collision, until at length he reached the much-desired
haven, the shelter of the gunboats at White House, on the Pamunkey River, after a skirmish there in which he was worsted.
At this point he crossed during the night, and was met by reinforcements, in connection with which he moved down the river,
and thence made for the Chickahominy, over which he passed
at the Forge Bridges. At Nance's Shop on June 24th (or Sa-
maria Church, as the fight is sometimes styled), he was struck
by Hampton: his line was charged by the dismounted men, who
handsomely carried the breast-works, and routed his command,
which was charged and pursued by two mounted regiments. It
was not until ten o'clock at night, and within two and a half
miles of Charles City Court House, that he was able by speed of
foot to shake off his pursuers, leaving behind, besides dead and

*Official Report of Gen. Hampton.

wounded, *157 prisoners. From this place he continued his retreat to Wyanoke Neck, and crossed the James River protected by his gunboats. Thus ended what is known as the "Trevylian Campaign," in which Sheridan was completely frustrated in the objects of his expedition, and driven by a force greatly inferior in numbers and *materiel* to his own, back to the cover of Grant's army. But if it had not been that on Saturday morning, June 11th, the right flank was uncovered—however, let us have done with "buts."

Gen. Hampton says† "the men could not have behaved better than they did" under "their hard marches, their want of supplies, their numerous privations." And it was not long afterwards that General Butler obtained the well-won stars of a Major-General.

Gen. Custer's report of the Trevylian campaign is interesting, one might almost say edifying. Usually his style in official reports is somewhat florid, suggestive of an imagination not unlike Rider Haggard's, such expressions as "driving the enemy," "routing them," "pursuit," &c., being of frequent occurrence. His account of the operations of June 11th, however, is a little toned-down from the customary manner, and what he says of June 12th is in a diction of chastened sobriety. From General Merritt's report it is learned that the force which Butler's Brigade first encountered in opening the fight on June 11th, was the celebrated "Second," and that the Senior Captain in command was wounded at an early hour that morning. Gen. Torbert, commanding First Division, reports that on the night of June 10th, just before going into camp, the head of his column was attacked by ten or twelve men, which was the first time any Confederates had been seen during the expedition. These were in fact Hampton's scouts. He also says that the next morning he could obtain no definite news of any enemy, until encountering their pickets. This information accords with that received from other sources, proving that Sheridan was completely surprised at Trevylian. Torbert wanders, however, into the region of romance, when he remarks that on June 12th the Confederate force was "reinforced by one or two regiments of infantry

---

*Gen. Gregg, commanding Second Division, admits being driven, and losing 357 men.
†Official Report of Gen. Hampton.

from Gordonsville." The reason given by him for the retreat that night is, that they had as many of their men wounded as they "could well take care of." Later on, in summing up the campaign to July, he observes, " When dismounted they (Confederates) have had a great advantage of us, from the fact that they have a very large Brigade of Mounted Infantry, armed with the rifled musket." To one with " a judicial mind" (as the newspapers say) it seems rather cool to call it an *advantage* to have muzzle-loaders against breech-loaders, but the remark is certainly a great compliment to the " long-shooters," and is an evidence of what a *bête noire* Butler's Brigade proved to those good people.

The impression derived from an examination of those portions of the reports of Sheridan's officers, which relate to the battle of Trevylian, cannot, I think, be otherwise than very unfavorable to the military reputation of that General. It is not necessary to " read between the lines " to find evidence of want of caution, resulting in the surprise of his force, and of lack of proper knowledge of the topography of the country, so that after crossing the river his Brigade Commanders were almost groping in the dark in their intended advance. It is clear that Custer arrived in the rear of Hampton's Division, not in the pursuance of any definite plan, but that he simply wandered into that position through the gap in the Confederate line on Fitz Lee's left. When, however, Custer by a fortunate accident found himself there, he tried to press his advantage, and it was then that Sheridan should have concentrated overwhelmingly on Hampton's Division, and destroyed it, while without support. But he failed to utilize the golden moments, showing himself unable to cope with the vigor of his antagonist. He consumed the remainder of Saturday in a series of isolated and spasmodic attacks, in which his troops were ably handled as far as tactics were concerned, and fought hard, but in a blind fashion, apparently without any strategical plan. The next day he must have taken a late Sunday morning nap, for it was not until the afternoon that he attacked, and in the meantime Fitz Lee was allowed ample opportunity to make a long detour, which was throughout plainly traceable by the dust-clouds, and thus reunite his command with that of Hampton.

The experience of an officer of the Fourth, who was taken pris-

oner at Trevylian, will serve to illustrate the precipitancy of
Sheridan's retreat. His rear guard began the march before day-
light, and at first some confusion was observable, due doubtless
to the supposed proximity of those villainous "long-shooters."
After a little while, however, there were no more signs of disorder, and during the remainder of the march good discipline
was manifest. This must be attributed in great measure to
the large leaven of regulars in the mass, whose technical train-
ing and habits of routine would be especially valuable at such a
time. The organization of the "Old Army" was perhaps the
most valuable asset of the dissolved Firm appropriated by the
Northern Partners; an asset to which, by some legerdemain of
reasoning, they became self-convinced they had of right an ex-
clusive claim, merely because the manufactory, founded and
maintained at the common expense, happened to be located at
West Point. The prisoners were compelled to walk hard to
keep pace with the rear-guard, and as cavalrymen are at best but
poor entries for a foot-race, it became necessary either to leave
behind many on the road-side temporarily exhausted, or to
give them occasional rests by dismounting regiments and putting Confederates in their saddles. The latter course was
adopted, not at all from motives of humanity, but to prevent
the loss of able-bodied prisoners, who, becoming in his keeping
living skeletons, or ghastly corpses, it mattered not which to
Secretary Staunton, represented so many rifles wrested from the
slender line of gray encircling, with hearts and hands, the Southern Cross. The march on the second day of the retreat (Tues-
day) was particularly hurried and distressing. One evening the
Confederate officers had been halted near a commodious, spa-
cious house on a large wheat plantation. It was a pretty home-
like scene, that quiet residence surrounded by a rolling country
with waving fields of "golden grain" and sweet flowering clover, and soft blue mountains in the far distance; by contrast
with their condition, it seemed to the jaded, half-dead prisoners
that they were

> " Full in the sight of Paradise,
> Beholding Heaven and feeling Hell!"

Just then a brisk little man came out of a small tent pitched
near the house, and, walking up to the group, saluted them civ-

illy in semi-military fashion, and said: "Gentlemen, I am sorry
to have been obliged to march you so hard, but it is unavoidable.
I have given orders that all the mattresses and bedding in this
house shall be spread on the floors of the rooms, so as to accom-
modate as many of you as possible, for you will require all the
rest you can get to enable you to stand the march to-morrow."
The speaker was "Phil Sheridan." On entering the building
the Confederates were met by the lady of the house, who apolo-
gized for having no food with which to give them a meal.
"They have taken every morsel on the place, even my little
children's supper," said she. This had been done, not in the
spirit of wanton destruction, but because the Federal troops pursued by Hampton were without rations, except some hard-tack,
coffee and sugar, which still remained in their wagons, and were
so closely pressed as to be unable to forage on the country in a
regular manner.

By the casualties of battle, and by illnesses contracted in the
service, the number of the Dragoons was now reduced to a very
small fraction of the aggregate on their muster-roll when they
marched for Virginia. What were left continued to do good
service under the command of Lieutenant Harleston during the
remainder of the summer. These participated in many skir-
mishes, and had much hard picketing. They did their part at
Ream's Station in August, where the cavalry covered themselves
with glory, and in the words of A. P. Hill, the General in command, "the sabre shook hands with the bayonet on the enemy's
captured breast-works." Early in October the Brigade was concerned in several affairs, in one of which General Dunnovant,
then commanding, was killed. It was during these fights that
Davis and Benjamin Bostick fell. F. R. Robertson, a bright
boy and a good soldier, also lost his life.

As the autumn came on men returned from wounded fur-
loughs, and reported for duty, and some new recruits or detached
men were also got into camp, so that a showing of a company
was kept up, though the ghost of its former self in numbers.*
When those who had been wounded came back, it was not always
as sound men, but their pluck nevertheless enabled them to act
the part of good soldiers. This was the case with Edward Now-

---

*During their term of Confederate service only two members of the company
died from causes other than wounds, or sufferings endured in Northern prisons.

ell, who was shot through the arm at Hawes' Shop, and who, in consequence, had one hand always in a partially crippled condition. Philip Hutchinson, wounded at Hawes' Shop, on his return became one of the scouts attached to the Cavalry Corps, in which capacity he did excellent service; an account of his adventures on the neutral ground between the two armies, and within the enemy's lines, would make a thrilling narrative.

At daylight on October 27th, the Brigade was compelled to leap into saddle very promptly, for the enemy were advancing heavy columns of infantry, having driven in and followed up closely the pickets; it was the commencement of the battle of Burgess' Mill. The cavalry had a tough time that morning skirmishing in different positions, fighting, too, on empty stomachs, which is "agin natur'." It was in this battle that a very deplorable event occurred. General Hampton, in riding along the lines that afternoon, happened to stop for a moment where the "Dragoons" were posted, and some members of his staff exchanged friendly words with acquaintances in the company. The General moved on, and within a very few minutes he had experienced a hair-breadth escape from death, and his two sons were wounded, one mortally. Major Barker, Divisional Adjutant, was also hit, and some couriers attached to Hampton's staff, were killed and wounded. At about three o'clock the Division settled down to a very brisk set-to with infantry of Hancock's corps, which continued until dark, just before which Lee flanked the Federals, who then withdrew. It was a heavenly sound, that preliminary growl, followed by a steady continous awe-inspiring roar of musketry, which announced that "Lee's foot-cavalry" were in force round the enemy's flank. It had been hot work, eighty rounds of ammunition having been that afternoon expended from the muzzle-loaders, which were not wasted, as proved by ghastly evidence next morning in the ground occupied by the Federals. Where the "Dragoons" were fighting the lines were less than 150 yards apart, separated by an open field, the opposing forces holding the edges of the woods on their respective sides. O'Brien (Tim O'Brien as he was always called) had been wounded at Hawes' Shop, and had reported back only a few days previously. He was not only a good soldier, but also one of the best tempered, most good natured men in the company, and of imperturbable coolness. In those days it used to be said jokingly, that it was good luck to be wounded, because one thus secured a furlough. O'Brien was fighting from behind a tree (oh! how *small* those trees did seem then), and, in drawing a bead on a blue-coat, was hit by a bullet. Realizing himself to be not critically injured, he cried out, imitating the negro dialect, "Tank yer Mausa, for gimme new furlough."

In December the Division, whose camp for a long time before had been near Stony Creek, moved to Bellefield (on the railroad to Weldon), where it was understood they were to go into winter quarters, keeping picket details some twelve or fifteen miles distant. A detachment from the "Dragoons" was on picket, when Grant in December made a demonstration, and reached Bellefield, but was driven back, chiefly by the cavalry, and that affair ended the campaign. The detail was compelled to remain on picket over a week. The men had been provided with rations for only four days, and could procure no other food, the weather was cold and stormy, and the videttes and posts were kept night and day in a constant state of disturbance by the enemy, who made feints on that part of the line to conceal his real object. As a consequence of all this the suffering endured was very great. When they returned to camp, however, at Bellefield, every one settled himself down for the winter, the only variation from the monotony of which was to be picketing. Some few flies were issued from the Quartermaster's Department, and one good sized "A" tent, which latter was used as Company head-quarters. Huger (Ben Huger) was at this time in command, Harleston being absent on sick-leave, and this tent was occupied by him and others. At Christmas a grand effort was made by Huger's mess to get up a feast: two of the members accordingly rode one day between thirty and forty miles foraging for this purpose, but so exhausted of supplies was the country in that vicinity, that they only succeeded in buying enough apple-brandy to fill a couple of canteens, one turkey, and few sweet potatoes. The apple-brandy had been kept in a barrel previously used for turpentine, which imparted to it a villainous flavor, but that was considered rather an advantage, for it made it last the longer. The turkey was purchased from two old women, who told the "Dragoons" they could have it, if able to catch it, which they evidently thought impracticable, and so it would have proved by ordinary means, but a revolver-bullet brought the coveted bird from his tree of safety, to the unbounded surprise and disgust of the women. A few days after Christmas a card-party was assembled in Huger's tent. The camp-fire burning outside had no effect in modifying the severity of the cold to those a few feet from it; so the fellows were wrapped in blankets; an old bayonet, taken from the enemy during their last demonstration, was stuck in the ground, the other end serving as socket for a tallow candle, and some corn borrowed from the horses was doing duty as "chips." A few sweet potatoes were in process of roasting under the ashes of the fire outside, and against the tent-pole was hanging a canteen with the remnant of the peculiar alcoholic compound above described. It was a gala-night, you will observe, and after the game there was to be a rare supper on the potatoes and the contents of the canteen. But the cards were suddenly thrown down, and the canteen prematurely called into requisition to drink with a will the toast "Home," for Julius Pringle, coming from Division Head-quarters, brought the glad tidings that Butler's and Young's Brigades, under command of Major-General Butler, had received orders to march for South Carolina. to rendezvous at Columbia, for the purpose of fighting Sherman.

The "Dragoons" reached Columbia with Butler's command, early in February. The town contained more than double the number of inhabitants it possessed when circumstances were normal. There were refugees congregated there from various places, chiefly from Sherman's line of march—old men, women, children, and the ill, bringing with them what little of value could be caught up in their flight from the destroyer. Some of the non-combatants, it is true, were persons engaged in commercial pursuits, striving to make money out of the necessities of the people, but these were mostly foreigners: there were very few "shirkers," and should have been none. A figure sometimes seen on the streets. always attracting involuntarily respectful observation, was Hon. Alfred Huger ("the Postmaster"): tall, erect, venerable. massive: dressed in homespun, but looking nevertheless as you would imagine an aged Senator to have appeared in the glorious years of Rome.

It is fruitless to recount the details of the skirmishing with Sherman's advance. All was done by Butler's Division that was practicable under the circumstances, and of course the "Dragoons" were to the front, but naturally no effectual resistance could be offered by a force of that size. If all available material had been handled with the same vigor as was used with this cavalry from the Army of Northern Virginia, the result of the subsequent campaign, in spite of the fearful odds, might have been different, although it was perhaps too late when Johnston assumed command at Charlotte.

The town of Columbia was without fortifications and ungarrisoned, and no defence of it, as a position, was attempted; there was merely skirmishing in the field with Sherman's advance. The place was only occupied by non-combatants, but yet the enemy shelled it as soon as he could reach it with his guns. About midnight of February 16th the "Dragoons" were withdrawn from the opposite side of the river, and waited in the town, near the end of the bridge, until morning, keeping their horses all the time saddled. The evacuation of the place, if the term can be correctly used of the mere retreat of troops through an unfortified and ungarrisoned city, commenced early in the morning of February 17th, Butler's (formerly) Brigade was the Confederate rearguard, and the "Dragoons," accompanying the General, followed at some little distance behind the Brigade. Just outside of the limits of the town, at a point near which the Charlotte Depot was then located, the road, or street, ascended a hill, from which a bird's-eye view of the town could be obtained. Here the "Dragoons," the company consisting of about twelve men, was halted, the rest of the rear-guard continuing their march and stopping some distance further on, quite beyond the limits of the city, so as to be able to cover the retreat of the main column and wagon-train. The Company was drawn up in column of fours on the brow of the hill, and although merely a handful of men, would appear to one looking from the ground below like the head of a body of considerable size. The orders given were, that if attacked no shots should be returned, but "fly at them with your sabres." It will be observed that these precautions were taken so as to prevent the possibility of a collision between the hostile forces occurring within the town, no Confederate soldier being then within its limits, and the civil authorities being in charge.

The "Dragoons" halted on the hill about ten o'clock, and remained there until near two, entirely unmolested except for six or eight shots from sharp-shooters, which were not returned. While there they watched Sherman's columns march into the city down a street at right angles to the road on which they were, and they could not fail to have seen fires, if any had occurred. There were then no fires having any connection whatever with the great conflagration ignited shortly after dark, which consumed the city, and the "Dragoons" were not withdrawn from their post of observation until hours after the formal surrender made by the Mayor had been accepted, and protection to private property promised. It is pleasant to have happened to be a witness to these facts. The destruction of Columbia, for no military purpose, a place which had been without fortifications or garrison, and undefended; which contained only noncombatants, and had been formally surrendered by the civil authorities; was a barbarous act utterly indefensible under the laws of war of all civilized nations. Sherman went to Columbia for the purpose of burning it, and there consummated a deliberately formed intention. The *evidence of this, from Federal as well as Confederate sources, is overwhelming. As for Sherman's statements to a contrary effect, their credibility is destroyed by (among other things) the fact of his saying in the same †page of his "Memoirs," that the conflagration " was accidental," and admitting that in his official report he " distinctly charged it to General Wade Hampton," and "did so pointedly, to shake the faith of his people in him." This extraordinary admission also shows what measure of reliance can be placed on some Federal official reports. If any one still has doubts as to the personality of the destroyer of Columbia, we must also remember that there are people living who do not believe Shakespeare wrote his own plays, and who think, for aught I know, that Napoleon Bonaparte was the author of Waverley. The contradictory " statements" remind one (as Mr. Lincoln would say) of a small darkey, who would persist invariably, " in season and out of season," in

---

*See sundry articles in Southern Historical Papers; Evidence before the Mixed Commission on Claims; Report of Committee appointed to collect Testimony in regard to Burning of Columbia; Article by Gen. Hampton in Baltimore Enquirer, June 24th, 1873, republished in Charleston Sunday News, February 5th, 1888, et cetera ad infinitum.

†Vol. 2d, page 287.

telling untruths, until at length his employer remonstrated:
"Ki! missus," replied he apologetically, "but dey does come
so slick off de tongue!"

It may naturally be supposed the "Dragoons" were in anything
but lively spirits, as they looked down upon the entrance of
Sherman into the city. Many of them were leaving behind
there near relatives, or dear friends; all were parting from kindly
acquaintances. As they had marched through the town many
a woman's pale face was seen at windows watching the retreating column, and no one with the heart of a man could feel
otherwise than pained and humiliated at being obliged to leave
under such circumstances. But it will often happen, on the
most solemn occasions, that some suggestion of the ludicrous
will intrude itself in a mal-apropos manner, mingling gro-
tesquely comedy and tragedy, and so it was at this time. One of
the "Dragoons" was wearing an overcoat of civilian style, an-
cient and wonderful in build, several sizes too large for him, and
utterly out of keeping with the rest of his dress, which gave him
a very droll appearance, and this was heightened by that of his
horse, a perfect Rosinante. This fellow was sincerely grieved at
the situation, but he also had a *magnum* of Madeira. He would
gaze towards the town, and the tears would roll down his cheeks,
his charger at the same time looking the picture of woe; then
he would slowly raise with both hands the huge bottle to his
lips, and take a pull, after which he would rest it again carefully on the pommel of his saddle, and resume the first part of
the programme. He was not at all intoxicated, and yet it was a
case of *in vino veritas*. It seemed well nigh sacrilegious to
waste such glorious wine in this and similar ways, but the owners
gave it away in preference to destroying it, fearing that otherwise drunkenness and excesses would result from its robbery by
Sherman's army. For days after this Madeira, shaken-up and
muddy, was being drunk along the road from tin-cups.

On the night of February 17th the Company rested, their
horses saddled and the men ready to mount instantly, within
about eight miles from Columbia. The next morning thick
clouds of smoke drifted past. The wind had been blowing in
an opposite direction until near daybreak, and when it changed
brought with it these indications of the fearful crime which had
been committed. As soon as it was definitely ascertained that

the town was burned, several "Dragoons" volunteered to return there disguised to learn the condition of the inhabitants, but their offer was not accepted.

The next day's march was to Winnsboro, and here Alfred Manigault was stricken down by a sudden attack of illness—a congestive chill, involving the brain. He had been far from well for some time previously, but his pluck had kept him in the saddle in spite of this; in the operations near Columbia he had been subjected to much exposure and hardship in scouting. He was left behind in hospital at Winnsboro when the command marched from there, and died some hours afterwards. His body was properly buried by the authorities, but when Sherman came up it was disinterred, and thus left on his departure.

The service entered upon by the "Dragoons" from this date was of a very exciting and not altogether disagreeable kind. They were detached from the Fourth Regiment, and were used by the Major-General commanding the Division as a body of couriers, and for special service, frequently in connection with himself personally. By this arrangement they avoided ordinary picket duty, but there was not a brush, that any portion of the Division had, in which they, or some of them, did not have a hand. There were but few days during which they were not under fire, and hitting back. There was much occupation in running down "bummers," and there is probably no other kind of warfare that contains such a source of sport. When flushed in small parties committing crimes, they would rarely show decent fight, but would run as if Satan himself was after them. Generally they were mounted on farm-animals stolen from the country people, and would be loaded with all kinds of family property, hams, bags of flour, women's dresses, children's clothes and play-things, clocks, &c. From time to time it may now be observed in the newspapers, that compunctions induce restitution to be made of articles of no intrinsic value thus stolen, but I have never noticed the return of watches, jewelry, or silver. It was amusing to see what wonderful speed a "bummer," fleeing from the wrath to come, could get out of an old mule loaded down with "booty." And then, as in spite of this the distance would be abridged between pursuer and pursued, it was diverting to watch the latter gradually lightening ship, first letting go a bag of flour, then a ham or two, and so on until at length perhaps the pious man would reluctantly throw overboard a family-bible. I suppose no occupation can be conceived of, except bummer-running, in which the delight of the sportsman, and the devotion and fervor of the Crusader are developed in the same individual at the same time. For you feel that if perchance you lose your life in thus defending and avenging women and children, you will go straight to Heaven. By "bummers" it is not meant to describe foragers, for foraging, legitimately conducted in an enemy's country to obtain necessary supplies for an army, is sanctioned by the laws of war; by "bummer" is meant a cowardly robber, and such were usually Sherman's so-called foragers. It would have been well had the robbery been confined to these, but unhappily it was being pursued systematically under the eyes of the Commanding General and his Staff. One of his *Military Family relates this: "It was comical," he says, to see the stealing of the personal effects and clothing of women and children. "Comical!" Defenceless women with their fatherless children crying to them in vain for bread! He observes that "the search made one of the excitements of the march." No wonder "bummer-running" was rare sport. And yet a †magazine for children, which is (or was) largely circulated at the South, coolly remarks that "American Boys and Girls," in reading their country's history, "will find no chapter more fascinating," than that which recounts the barbarities of Sherman's march. However, we will no more vex the reader's and our own soul by dwelling on this subject or describing the track of fire visible night and day. One incident (a mild case) may serve as a description of bummer-running. On the march between Winnsboro and Cheraw, it happened one morning that a small detachment, pursuing a somewhat unfrequented road, came suddenly upon a so-called foraging party of the enemy. In front of a small farm-house stood the cart belonging to the owner, which the "foragers" had loaded with everything from the house that they fancied, and they were, when pounced upon, in the very act of setting fire to the building, the women and children, whose only shelter it was, having taken to the woods to avoid a worse fate. The cart was loaded with hetero-

---

*" Story of the Great March from the Diary of a Staff Officer," by Major George Ward Nichols, Aide-de-Camp to Sherman.

†St. Nicholas, May, 1887.

geneous articles, making a pyramid eight or nine feet in height, on the very top of which was a large family-bible. The house stood at a point where the road forked at an acute angle, and by dashing through the woods and thus saving distance, some of the Confederates were able to cut off "bummers" who had fled down the other road at their approach, and also to have fine sport chasing these worthies mounted on all manner of four-footed animals loaded down with plunder. Yells and cheers, pistol-shots and halloos, mingled in a wild chorus as that race for life was run. On returning from the chase one of the men took a short-cut near the fork of the roads, and was riding through some long thick broom-grass, when, almost from under his horse's feet, up jumped an officer and begged for his life. He protested that he had been *taking a nap*, and was quite igno-rant of and horrified at the conduct of his soldiers, poor inno-cent.

Frequently attacks on "bummers" would be of a more serious nature. Such was the case early one rainy morning at Cantey's Farm, on Lynch's Creek D——, a scout, who had been attached to the Division in Virginia, and had accompanied the command to South Carolina, came galloping in on his little bay horse (or more properly speaking pony), and reported about 200 infantry "foragers" engaged in pillaging the house and out-buildings preparatory to applying the torch.

"They have stacked their arms in the yard," said he, "and you can bag every one of them, and get off before reinforce-ments can arrive."

So Colonel Rutledge with the Fourth was ordered forward for this purpose.

Now, after leaving the main road the approach to Cantey's had to be made down a lane, or avenue, nearly a half mile in length, which led to the farm-yard where the Federals had stacked arms, and near which they were busy plundering. In traversing this lane the Fourth would be in plain view, but by riding quietly along on a walk, talking and laughing, with sheathed sabres and pistols in the holsters, it was thought the "bummers" would mistake the Confederates for their own people, especially as the men in the head of the column wore blue over-coats captured from the enemy in Virginia. This plan was car-ried out, and worked capitally. Every now and then some of the " foragers " would come out of the house, look at the party approaching, and then return within doors in fancied security.

"They think we are Kilpatrick's men," quietly remarked D——, who was riding beside Col. Rutledge. D—— was a rather small person, inoffensive in appearance, light in weight, and wiry, but not athletic in build. His manners were excellent, and the tones of his voice habitually gentle. But he was like a blood-hound on the trail of human blood, and a very devil in action: a wonderful pistol-shot, seldom missing even when at full speed. The transformation from the man's natural disposition to his acquired proclivities was caused in this way. He was a native of the " Valley of Virginia," whose fertile fields, picturesque streams and beautiful mountains, rendered famous by the genius of Stonewall Jackson, had been the witnesses of much ruthless devastation. He was the sole survivor of five brothers. The three oldest of these had met soldiers' deaths in defending their home. The youngest, a high-spirited boy of sixteen, had joined a cavalry company, and with his mother's kisses and tears still almost wet on his cheeks, had been killed. A dash had been made into Winchester, and in retreating the boy's horse had fallen when turning a corner. While the child was lying injured and helpless on the ground, he was butchered by Federal mercenaries (Thank God ! not by *Americans!*). From that moment D—— was a changed man; he vowed that he would die, or score twenty-five dead Federals for every brother he had lost. The count stood at several over seventy, when he himself was disabled by a wound; I know nothing of his subsequent career. The day after he had been shot in the leg, I saw him charge "bummers," having thrown the injured limb over the pummel of his saddle in "lady fashion." After that the wound became worse, and being unable to ride, he then offered to give his little horse to one of the " Dragoons," by far the greatest compliment the latter ever received. D—— was a very interesting character, which must be the justification for this digression.

At length, when the Fourth had reached to within a few yards of the house, a "bummer" shouted something to his friends, and immediately they all made a rush for their arms. But most of them were too late, for Rutledge shouted " Charge !" and the Fourth made quick clean work. But as for D——, like a tiger on his prey, horse and rider sprang among them, and as rapidly as you could fire a "right and left" at partridges, two "bummers" lay dead (he had a knack of *killing*, not *wounding*); he scored a third just afterwards, and more for aught I know. As for the other Federals, not many escaped, for there were open fields around and behind the house extending a considerable distance, which afforded the cavalry a fair chance for such pell-mell business.

At Cheraw a junction was made with troops from the former garrisons of Charleston and Savannah. These were withdrawn across the Pee Dee River in consequence of the approach of Sherman's large force, Butler's Division being the rear-guard. The "Dragoons" remained in the town covering the removing of pickets. While this was being done, and they were in column of twos, the Federals managed to bring up a gun to fire down the main street, in which they were at that time stationed. The Company was accordingly ordered to wheel round and take a street at right angles, so as to avoid the line of fire As this was being done, one of the "Dragoons" rode up on his return from delivering to a picket-post an order of withdrawal, and joined the rear rank of the company. He had just taken his place, when the gun opened fire, and the first shot, a rifled-shell, struck his horse in the rear, and passed out between the front legs without exploding, leaving the poor animal nearly disemboweled. The rider was unhurt, but had some difficulty in disentangling himself from his dead horse, which, however, he lost no time in doing, for he was mentally calculating how many seconds would be required to reload the gun, feeling sure it would be fired from the same position, and that the projectile would strike in identically the same spot as the last. Freed from the horse, he hastily snatched up his few effects easily removable, but as the saddle and bridle were under the carcass of the animal, and therefore not to be got without some delay, he concluded to leave them behind, as a contribution to the cause of the Union, and to rejoin his company, which by this time had filed round the corner. Gen. Butler, however, had remained in the street watching the artillerymen, and when he saw the "Dragoon" was about to leave, remarked quietly, pointing to the saddle and bridle, "Don't you think you will have some further use for those things?" The hint was of course at once taken, and never before were saddle and bridle removed from horse, dead or alive, so quickly, the man meanwhile expecting each second there would be a collision with a shell in which he would play a prominent part. Hardly were they taken off, when the considerate gentlemen at the other end of the street let fly another messenger of peace and good will, which came along shrieking and talking through its nose, struck a pump standing in the middle of the roadway by the corner, and then carromed into a house, fortunately without hurting any one. At this the Dragoon observed, " I've got my saddle and bridle, General, but I'm damned if I want the *halter*," and then made the best of his way round the corner.

Besides the skirmishing and bummer-running, there were occasionally more important affairs of the cavalry during this campaign. Such was the surprise of Kilpatrick's camp, some eight miles from Fayetteville, N. C., on March 10th, which has already been *described in some detail. A picket sent out by Kilpatrick to occupy a road was captured, noiselessly, without the firing of a shot, by General Butler, his Staff and the Dragoons being the force with which this feat was performed. The night closed in dark and rainy, and this good fortune was availed of to surprise and route the entire Federal Cavalry Corps before sunrise the next morning. The day preceding this brilliant affair was very wet, and the roads over which Kilpatrick's corps passed were much cut-up by vehicles. During that afternoon, on striking such a road, a Confederate detachment noticed the track of wheels looking very unlike the broad ruts left by artillery, or wagon-trains. These impressions were evidently those made by a light carriage, and not by some coarse " buggy " stolen from the country people. Then there arose much excitement among certain of the " Dragoons;" they opened in full cry on the trail in fact. Indeed there were not wanting some older fellows, who smiled and looked interested. To make clear the cause of all this it will only be necessary to give this explanation. At Columbia, prior to February 17th, might have been seen, any day and many times a day, a certain very pretty woman, " dressed to kill," driving in her carriage, her dainty little feet rarely touching the pavement except when she was entering a shop. She did not belong to the *demi monde*, or the " Dragoons," being properly behaved young men, of course would not have been acquainted with her; yet it must be confessed her paternity, like that of some of the most famous Goddesses of Mythology, was involved in much obscurity. This damsel, under her mother's wing, left Columbia with Sherman's army, and afterwards made an advantageous marriage at the North with a relative of a noted Brooklyn preacher, who was by profession a philanthropist, in practice a philogynist. After skirmishing a little while in the borderland of Gotham's society, she figured as defendant in a law suit; then indulged in pistol-practice in the streets, lodging a derringer-bullet among the back teeth of one of the *jeunesse dorée*, and finished up by marrying a second time a titled foreigner of Latin extraction. Now these wheel-tracks were supposed to have been made by the carriage of this beautiful Helen of Troy, and she herself was believed to be in Kilpatrick's camp, where unprotected females were wont to find a haven. The cause of the excitement among the boys, and their elders, too, probably needs no further explanation. When, therefore, afterwards the picket was captured, and the attack upon Kilpatrick was arranged, it may well be imagined that the delight of the youngsters was unbounded. As wet, hungry and tired, they passed that night sitting on the ground, each man with his bridle-rein through his arm, ready to mount at command; with no fires or smoking, or conversation allowed, lest the enemy detect something wrong; their troubled dreams probably ran more on those wheel-tracks than on the hard fight against many times their number, which was in store for them before sun-rise. It is a glorious thing to be young and without responsibilities; to have a strong constitution and a good conscience.

By the first dim light of a foggy morning, the detachment, to which had been assigned the first charge, thundered through Kilpatrick's camp. If an earthquake had burst upon them, the Federals could not have been more astonished and demoralized. At first they did not attempt to fight, but made-off in every direction, leaving behind their accoutrements. All the "Dragoons" rode into the camp in the rear of the detachment which first charged, except William Fishburne, who had been sent forward to deliver a message to some one, and having performed this duty, fell-in with the charging column, having a marked

proclivity for always being in fights.   Just to the right of where
the " Dragoons " entered was a small farm-house, which proved
to be Kilpatrick's head-quarters, but at that moment unfortunately this was not understood.   A good many horses were tied
near this house, and some of the men about there fought hand-
to-hand for awhile, so that it was like a ball at which one could
obtain a vis-a-vis readily.   While this was going on, a rather
rough dirty looking person, clothed only in shirt and drawers,
without boots or hat, rushed frantically out of the house, cut
the halter of a horse tied to a post of the piazza, jumped upon
the animal bare-backed, and sped away as if upon a "quarter-
race."   This individual was unknown, and therefore was allowed to escape, but it was Kilpatrick.   Some little time afterwards there stepped forth from the house a figure, which made
a sensation—a lone damsel.   At the first flutter of the dress and
sight of the round straw-hat, the boys thought their hopes were
realized, but a nearer view dashed them: it was not the beautiful siren with the wonderful blonde hair, of whom they had
been dreaming: the romance had vanished.   This female character who thus made her appearance in the performance, was a
rather plain looking and not over-young person.   She had been,
it was said, a "school-marm" from Vermont, but with the ver-
satility of her people, on finding that occupation did not "pay"
well, had turned to temporarily presiding over Kilpatrick's military establishment.   Her urgent wish on this occasion was that
her horses should be harnessed to the carriage, but as that was
impracticable, and she was incurring great risk of being accidentally shot, some one persuaded her to lie down in a drainage-
ditch on the road-side, which, like a sensible woman, she did,
and thus was unhurt by the bullets.   But it was a sad pity that
much of the romance of the adventure was spoiled by lack of
attractiveness in the heroine.   As for the Division, acting in
connection with a part of Gen. Wheeler's men, after the first
surprise and route of Kilpatrick's Corps had been effected, as
described, it drove the demoralized cavalrymen pell-mell back to
the protection of a large body of infantry, and then withdrew,
carrying away nearly as many prisoners as the entire number of
the attacking force, besides much materiel and many horses,
including three which had been "appropriated" along the line
of march by the Federal General.   All the Confederate prisoners

held by Kilpatrick, consisting chiefly of stragglers and the sick from the infantry, were released. A tragic incident in connection with this occurred. Two poor fellows, on first seeing the Confederate columns, broke from the Federal Provost guard, and rushed forward with frantic cheers, welcoming their deliverers, but in the fog and powder-smoke were mistaken for charging enemies, and were killed.

At Fayetteville an affair occurred in which the "Dragoons" again figured prominently. Their Division was the rear-guard in the crossing of the Cape Fear River, but the Company had gone to the town early in the morning to await there the arrival of the command, for the purpose of crossing after it had passed over the bridge. There was something in the place that was called a hotel, and the "Dragoons" had leave to get breakfasts there, if practicable, while awaiting the arrival of the Division. This did not prove possible however for three of them, as there was not sufficient breakfast to "go round," and what there was naturally became appropriated by the "higher dignitaries." So the three troopers with empty stomachs were "cooling their heels" on the outside of the hotel, listening to the enlivening clatter made by the weapons of the "valiant trenchermen" within, and waiting for "their turn," when their attention was attracted by a fellow galloping past, as if he had a very pressing engagement elsewhere. They hailed him to ask what he was in such a hurry about, but without slackening speed he pointed with his thumb over his shoulder, muttering something, which seemed to be "jist thar." From this it was inferred that something was wrong; so the three "Dragoons" mounted and rode round the corner in the direction indicated, and "jist thar" they were, sure enough, a mounted company of *seventy-five Federals drawn up in the street in column of fours.

Now this was, or might become, a serious situation. It was not to be supposed that the detachment was distant from its supports, such not being the habit of Kilpatrick's troopers, and it was therefore presumably the advance-guard of a much larger body. Nearly all the Confederate force had by this time crossed the bridge, but a part, including Butler's Division, was still on the Southern side of the river, and it looked as if the enemy

---

*The Captain (named Duncan, I think), who was captured, stated this to be the number.

was about to attempt to cut-off the latter, which was still some distance from the town. Moreover, by preventing the burning of the bridge, the Federals would be able to press the retreating Confederate columns, which had already crossed.

The three " Dragoons " had not been long in the street, and one was about returning to report to head-quarters, when Gen. Hampton galloped round the corner, accompanied by either three or four followers, and a few seconds afterwards gave the order " Charge !" And at them the eight (or seven) rushed in full speed, yelling, as if pealing " the banner-cry of Hell," and shooting their pistols into the mass. The Federals fired one volley with carbines, but before they had time for doing more, the Confederates were within a few feet of the head of their column, against which they would have dashed at the full run, if to avoid the collision, the entire company had not broken and fled. For their own good they ought either to have left sooner, or to have stood more firmly, for, as it was, they could not have managed the matter better for their foes, who, striking them at close quarters when broken, had after that mere bummer-running, not fighting, the sabres doing good work when the pistols were emptied. The bag, as counted, amounted to eleven, but no doubt some more escaped wounded. The result was that the enemy did not make any further attempt to press with cavalry, and the Confederates crossed the bridge unmolested, except the very last, who exchanged some compliments with sharp-shooters. The Captain in command of the Federals was not with his company when it was attacked, but was captured plundering in a house near by. On the body of one of the killed were found several watches, besides a considerable sum of money. The Confederates lost no men, but one gallant horse received a bullet in the chest, which passed out behind the girth, and yet he showed no symptoms of distress until after the fight and pursuit were ended, when his weakness gave the first intimation that he had received a mortal wound. The service rendered by the three " Dragoons " on this occasion was thought at the time by Gen. Hampton to merit marked commendation, and he accordingly wrote an official communication to that effect to Lieutenant Harleston, commanding the Company, in which document he says they " acted with conspicuous gallantry in charging and

driving from the town of Fayetteville that party of the enemy's
cavalry which entered the town before it had been evacuated by
our troops. Their conduct on this occasion reflects high credit
upon them as soldiers."

At Smithfield the army halted, and here the " Dragoons " reported back to the Fourth Regiment as Co. K. Some of them
had been wounded during the campaign, but none had been
killed. Their number had at this time been increased by fresh
recruits, and by members returned from sick or wounded fur-
loughs, as well as by some absentees resurrected from Bureau-
details. Not long afterwards a detachment of four men under
Lieutenant Harleston, was ordered to the adjoining County
(Nash), to collect horses. They found a country not only literally " over-flowing with milk and honey," but with " peach and
honey" as well. The people were kindly, but withal not warri-
ors. There were comparatively a large number of able-bodied
men there, who, by hook, or by crook, had evaded military service. One of these, in describing some absent friend, for whom
he evidently entertained a great admiration, became for a moment at a loss for a simile to properly illustrate the courage he
attributed to his hero: " He is as brave as — as," he hesitated a
moment, "as—a *Oxen*." One need not entertain doubt as to
what manner of men these were, who could suppose the highest
courage typified by "*a Oxen !*"

In April riding along a road one morning some cavalrymen
were met coming from the North. " How is this ? Where are
you from ?" was asked of the strangers. They replied that they
were from the Army of Northern Virginia; that Lee had surrendered, and they were in consequence returning to their homes
paroled. Then " Liars ! Cowards ! Deserters !" were some of
the vile epithets hurled contemptuously at these men, for was it
not impossible, and a foul thing not even to be whispered in
Heaven, or Earth, or Hell, that Lee's Army could surrender !
They bore the abuse in silence, and passed on their way. Soon
afterwards a larger party was encountered, with which were several officers, and the " Dragoons " discovered then that they had
been unjustly reviling as good as, indeed better men than themselves for these were paroled soldiers, who had borne " the
agony and bloody sweat" of a terrible crucifixion; who had only

reluctantly ceased fighting against incredible odds at Lee's bidding.

The " Dragoons," who were with the army, were surrendered by Johnston. They were formed in line, and the momentous news announced. Hutchinson (Philip Hutchinson), who had done notably good service at Pocotaligo, had been wounded at Hawes' Shop, and had afterwards, as already related, performed severe duty as a scout, burst into tears, threw his hat passionately on the ground, and spoke wild words; there were many instances of the same kind.

The detachment in Nash County did not surrender for many weeks afterwards, but rode through the country Southward, as best they could, passing by towns and settled neighborhoods at night. getting little food for man or beast, intending to renew the fight under the Southern Cross in the Trans-Mississippi Department, where they understood the war would still be waged. But it was not to be: the war was ended, and with the extinction of the mighty Confederate Armies, the Charleston Light Dragoons, small in numbers, insignificant in material strength, but of unquenchable courage and unsullied honour, ceased to exist.

The principles for which the Confederates fought, were, beyond question, legally and morally right. In their behalf brilliant genius and unsurpassed valor, the manhood of the country from highest to lowest, had charged shoulder to shoulder: together had endured hunger and thirst, cold and heat, wounds and death: together had won victories, whose glory will be immortal. Then why, in the name of the just God; why was the cause at last overwhelmed? Why did eternal right sink before mere numerical might ? This is a problem impossible of solution, but one thing is certain: in the destruction of the independence of the Southern States was struck the most injurious blow against Civil Liberty, against the principle that Governments among English-speaking peoples derive "their just powers from the consent of the governed." which has been dealt in modern times. The effects of this we may feel sure the world will have reason yet bitterly to deplore, and must expunge " with blood and iron," unless " the mills of the Gods " change their immemorial manner of grinding. Conscious of rectitude in the past, confident of vindication in the future, we

"Furl that Banner! True, 'tis gory,
  Yet 'tis wreathed around with glory,
  And 'twill live in song and story,
    Though its folds are in the dust:
  For its fame on brightest pages,
  Penned by poets and by sages,
  Shall go sounding down the Ages,—
    Furl its folds though now we must."

After returning to their homes (or what was left of them) at the end of the war, the remaining members of the Charleston Light Dragoons formed themselves into a Survivors' Association. The objects of the organization were to preserve, by continued personal association, the friendships existing between the men, to dispense charity, as far as practicable, to the families of comrades, and eventually to erect a Monument to their fallen fellow-soldiers. All of these purposes were accomplished, the last being consummated under difficulties, solely through the voluntary contributions of members, and of the relatives of their dead. The Monument, at Magnolia Cemetery, consists of an obelisk hewn from native granite, a form which has been used in all times to symbolize, among other meanings, undying life, and in this sense it was selected by the "Dragoons." It signifies, for them, the imperishable nature of Civil Liberty, and the immortality of the souls of their comrades, who, "across the River," now "rest under the shade of the trees," and proclaims the indestructible love cherished for Confederate Soldiers by all of their countrymen worthy of the name.

During 1876, the year of the State's redemption, and prior to that date, a Sabre Club existed here under the title of the Charleston Light Dragoons. Those were the days of Grant's Presidential administrations, when Law and Order were overturned under a spurious State Government unlawfully erected by Federal force, and by it only sustained. Hordes of ignorant

negroes, and corrupt carpet-baggers, and a few infamous rene-
gades, were banded together against the manhood and woman-
hood of the country: these " *hostes humani generis,*" self-styled
State Militia, were armed with rifles furnished from Washington. To keep alive the almost extinguished spark of civiliza-
tion, the Rifle and Sabre Clubs were instituted under the man-
agement of Confederate Soldiers, and were maintained in spite
of "proclamations." In this movement the Charleston Light
Dragoon Sabre Club bore an honorable part. On the setting-up
of a real State Government, under the leadership of Hampton
and Butler, this Club became a Militia Company, and to its cus-
tody the Survivors' Association afterwards confided in perpetu-
ity their completed Monument. To this post-bellum body the
Survivors of the War-corps have given their sympathy and best
wishes, and in it they have been much pleased to accept the
kindly tendered positions of Honorary Members. We are confident that when in the future comes the day. as come among all
peoples it must; when again the ground shall shake under the
impact of thousands of hoofs marshaled in the terrible, but magnificent array of battle; then the name of the Charleston Light
Dragoons will be borne by true Soldiers, who, be they few, or
many, will war to the death for Eternal Right.

LIST OF THE NAMES OF THE DEAD ON THE MONUMENT.

——— —

JAMES W. O'HEAR, *Lieutenant.*
J. ALLEN MILES, *Sergeant.*
ALFRED MANIGAULT, *Corporal.*
CHARLES E. PRIOLEAU, *Corporal.*
ARTHUR ROBINSON, *Corporal.*

James Adger, Jr.
Josiah Bedon.
James L. Bee.
J. H. W. Boone.
Benjamin Bostick.
James Creighton.
W. R. Davis.
W. H. Fairly.
A. C. Frierson.
T. G. Holmes.
W. L. Kirkland.
Thomas Lining.
T. S. Marion.
W. W. McLeod.
F. K. Middleton.
O. H. Middleton, Jr.
T. W. Mordecai, Jr.
Edward W. Nowell.
J. J. A. O'Neill.
A. B. Phillips.
Percival R. Porcher.
J. R. P. Pringle.
Alexander Robertson, Jr.
Eber R. Robertson.
Louis M. Vander Horst.

www.ingramcontent.com/pod-product-compliance
Lightning Source LLC
Chambersburg PA
CBHW032200010726
47493CB00008BA/2770